Under the Naked Sky

D0840016

Short Stories
from the *Arab World*

Under the Naked Sky

Short Stories
from the *Arab World*

Selected
and translated by
Denys Johnson–Davies

The American University in Cairo Press
Cairo • New York

First published in Egypt in 2000 by
The American University in Cairo Press
113 Sharia Kasr el Aini, Cairo, Egypt
420 Fifth Avenue, New York, NY 10018
www.aucpress.com

First paperback edition 2003

Dar el Kutub No. 19205/02
ISBN 978 977 424 780 4

    3 4 5 6 7 8 9 10 11 12   12 11 10 09 08 07

Designed by Andrea El-Akshar/AUC Press Design Center
Printed in Egypt

Contents

Contents

vi

Introduction

As long ago as 1946 I published, at my own expense in Cairo, a small volume of short stories. It was a selection from the work of Mahmoud Teymour, described by critics as "the pioneer of the Arabic short story," and was, I believe, the first volume of Arabic short stories to be published in English translation.

While in Cairo I had come to know other writers such as Naguib Mahfouz and Yahya Hakki, and had also read what I considered worthwhile stories by non-Egyptian writers. I therefore started to collect material for a book that would be representative of the short story in the Arab world as a whole. The project dragged on as I read widely on the recommendation of such writers as Jabra Ibrahim Jabra, a Palestinian friend from my Cambridge days who had been forced out of his home in Bethlehem and had settled in Baghdad. I often found myself translating a story that, I was forced to admit, either I had misjudged or that had irrevocably suffered in its transition from Arabic to English. Finally, I made up a volume of twenty stories and began the thankless task of trying to find a London publisher. I was under no illusions about the difficulty of finding a home for the volume I had produced but nevertheless felt that somewhere there must be an adventurous publisher who would take on the book, a book that at least had the novelty of introducing a whole new area of writing. The task proved as difficult as I had envisaged and the manuscript was about to be confined to a drawer when an acquaintance suggested that I send it to a friend of his at the unlikely venue of the Oxford University Press. My delight knew no bounds when I received a letter from this illustrious academic publishing house to say that they would be prepared to publish the volume of stories—provided I could persuade a leading Arabist to write an introduction to it. In reply I protested that the translation of a volume of stories was not a work of scholarship. The publishers, however, insisted, so I wrote to A. J. Arberry, Professor of Arabic at Cambridge, whom I knew slightly. He generously agreed, despite being in poor health and pointing out that he was not a specialist in modern Arabic literature.

The volume duly appeared under the title *Modern Arabic Short Stories* in 1967—not an auspicious year for the first ever book of stories from the Arab world. It did not sell well and received scant attention in the press. I later included it in the Arab Authors series that I had started with Heinemann, from where it was taken by an American publisher and later by the American University in Cairo Press. It is thus, over thirty years later, still in print.

Egyptian writers in that volume included Naguib Mahfouz, Yusuf Idris, Yahya Hakki, and Edwar al-Kharrat. The Mahfouz story, "Zaabalawi," was to find its way into the prestigious pages of Norton's *Great Masterpieces of the World*, as the only example of Arabic writing apart from some extracts from the Quran and others from the *Arabian Nights*—and this before the author was awarded the Nobel Prize. Other outstanding stories in the volume were "The Doum Tree of Wad Hamid" by the Sudanese writer Tayib Saleh—presaging his novella *The Wedding of Zein* and his widely read *Season of Migration to the North*. Palestine was represented by stories from Ghassan Kanafani and Jabra Ibrahim Jabra; Lebanon by one of the two women writers in the volume, Laila Baalabaki, and Iraq by Abdel Malik Nouri and Fuad al-Takarli; from Syria there were stories by Abdel Salam al-Ujeili and Walid Ikhlassi, also by the young Zakaria Tamer, who was to become one of the most prolific and skilled practitioners of the genre.

In 1983 I produced a second volume of *Stories from the Arab World* (so named to distinguish it from the OUP volume), in which I incorporated writers from North Africa (Mohamed Chukri and Mohamed Barrada from Morocco, Habib Selmi from Tunisia, and Ibrahim al-Koni fom Libya), also younger writers from Egypt such as Ibrahim Aslan and Mohamed El-Bisatie, the late Yahya Taher Abdullah and the talented Iraqi Mohamed Khudayir, as well as the Lebanese writer Hanan al-Shaykh, who has made an international name for herself as a novelist. Here again, the collection remains in print.

And now, with a volume incorporating more names than the previous ones, I am seeking to bring the picture of the Arabic short story up to date. One difference that may be noted in the present volume is that it includes more stories by women writers than in the previous collections—no less than eight out of a total of thirty stories. As in the previous volumes, I have preferred to choose writers who are still alive. In this, though, I have made three exceptions: a very short and little-known story by the acknowledged leader of the form in Egypt, Yusuf Idris; a story by the Jordanian writer Ghalib Halasa, who by rights I should have included in the 1983 volume; and a story by the Saudi Arabian writer Abd al-Aziz Mishri, who died a matter of days after I translated it. Although the present volume contains more stories than either of the two earlier volumes, the job of making my final choice was this time very much harder. In the 1960s the writers of short stories were limited in number and more or less known. Between then and now the number of those seeking to make a name for themselves in this field has grown prodigiously: to such an extent that a Cairene wit remarked that if one were to go up in a helicopter over Talaat Harb Square and drop a brick, one would be sure to hit a writer of short stories! The same applies throughout the Arab world. In making my choice for this volume I have not attempted to represent all of the many countries making up the Arab world but have been guided by my own liking for certain stories regardless of their provenance. Almost certainly, some stories of real worth have escaped my net or have been dropped for want of space; other stories I may have considered to present particular difficulties for the non-Arab reader. All I can hope for is that the selection more or less represents those writers who are considered the best of those currently practicing this genre, with here and there a writer who is perhaps less well known but whose story particularly appealed to me.

For the purposes of collecting the material for this book, I read many hundreds of short stories. I was saved from yet further reading by several friends who helped me by suggesting the names of writers with whose work I was not acquainted and individual stories that might meet my requirements. Among such I would number in particular: Mohamed El-Bisatie, Said al-Kafrawi, Yusuf Abu Rayya, Mahmoud Al-Wardani, Ferial Ghazoul, Salwa Bakr, and the artist Adel al-Siwi (who has also contributed the jacket illustration) from Egypt; Ibrahim Samoueil from Syria; the novelist and poet Ibrahim Nasrallah from Jordan; the writer and editor Khalid al-Maali from Germany; and the poet and artist Maysoun Saqr and the poet and scholar Ahmed Rashid Thani from the United Arab Emirates.

Finally, my thanks to Neil Hewison for once again editing a text by me with his usual efficiency and tact.

The Pilot

Mohamed Makhzangi

Aboard a slim boat among the forests of reeds at the lake's edge I stood watching what was happening. I was using binoculars to observe this method of hunting duck, though without really believing my eyes. It seemed to me a simple, unnatural contrivance, aptly named 'submersion.' The noses of the hunters practicing it reminded me of the Hyksos. I knew that long ago they had infiltrated to this spot, settling on the lake shore. The memory of Tanis, submerged somewhere in the water in front of me, gave me the idea that something unpleasant would perhaps repeat itself. I jeered at the sight of the hunter I was following getting his equipment ready: tying his pocket knife by the handle to a string dangling from his wrist, he put on his cap made of leather and duck feathers and began to push his way into the water. He submerged himself up to his nose. In the middle of the lake it looked as if a wild duck were swimming about. But it was a very poor sort of a duck, a travesty of a duck for anyone giving it a moment's scrutiny.

The flight of duck wove into sight on the lake's horizon, led by the drake, the pilot. The flight advanced like a large dark arrowhead against the clear, luminous surface of the sky. It seemed to me something sublimely cosmic in its sweep. But I felt ill at ease when I saw it suddenly changing course from winging its way in the heavens to dipping down toward the water, toward the fake swimming bird. It was with a trembling heart that I waited for the eyes of the pilot bird to grasp the sheer crudity of the deception. There was no doubt that this might occur, be it at the very last moment. But the pilot bird did not turn back and the arrow carried on in its descent. All at once I heard the splash as the feet and bellies of the birds came into contact with the water. The arrow put down on the waters of the lake, becoming a triangle of closely packed birds, with the ambush lying in the very heart of the triangle.

The birds close to the fake duck gave out a small collective pulsation. In a flash one of them vanished, leaving in its place a gap that was quickly filled by the closely packed birds. The Hyksos hunter in this flash of time gently stretched out his hand under the water, catching hold of the feet of the duck nearest him. Pulling it under the water before it could cry out or struggle, he busied himself with cutting its throat. Then he tied it by the feet to the belt around his waist so that it hung down, trailing blood.

The birds were quickly dwindling in number. I was astonished that they were not alarmed by their startling reduction in number or by the water around them becoming stained with blood.

It was clear that the Hyksos hunter made a point of leaving the leader, the pilot bird, to the end. The other birds, as they diminished in number, would move automatically to crowd together again, retaining the shape of a triangle, with the pilot bird at its apex. It became apparent to me that in their long flight and when they were swimming, the birds never looked around them. It was enough for each to keep its mind on where the pilot was and to follow it. Flying in arrowhead formation and crowding together into a triangle were merely instinctive measures to allow each bird to have a commanding view of the pilot. Seeing the pilot, each bird is reassured. Whether its neighbor vanishes or remains in place, nothing worries the bird so long as the pilot is there: the pilot flies and the bird flies behind, the pilot alights and the bird too alights. The Hyksos hunter no doubt understood this, so would leave the pilot alone. Did the pilot not notice?

But how should the pilot notice? As I watched it through my binoculars for a long time, it looked neither around nor behind itself. It seemed to look out only for itself, just so long as it felt that there was a bird of like species following it. But the bird that remained was not following it—there was only the cap of the Hyksos hunter, hidden under the water, that travesty of a duck that jumped to his feet with a cry of total victory. This time the hunter did not drag his prey under the water to cut its throat. He grasped hold of it, keeping it alive. But what sort of a life for the pilot bird in the grasp of the hunter, who had emerged exultantly from the bloodied water, around his middle the bodies of the rest of the birds, swinging by their tied feet, the slaughtered covey that was?

It's Not Fair

Yusuf Idris

We had a friend called Abdul Magid, whose very name was synonymous with hashish. One of the few real connoisseurs of the stuff, his experience of it was both vast and various. While we always found him permanently high, we could also be sure that his pocket invariably housed yet further reserves.

Many were the days when Abdul Magid became for us an endless topic of conversation. He was a man whose every word was a joke, his every retort a play on words, and at the mere mention of his name each of us was able to recount tens of stories about his experiences with Abdul Magid or his antics.

Abdul Magid worked as a doctor at a large hospital. While most people believe that doctors are necessarily short, stoutly-built, pot-bellied, and thick-necked and that they wear spectacles and a benign air, Abdul Magid was quite the opposite, being tall, lean, and of a pallid complexion.

But I don't want to digress about Abdul Magid (which would be only too easy), for his life story was like that of life itself:

having found a beginning to it, one never succeeded in discovering an end.

The point of our story is that he was once on night duty and had to stay awake in readiness for the various accidents the city would be hatching. He was not one to let such an occasion pass without making the very minutest preparations for it. He had therefore smoked until his eyes, though not white, were not yet red but had become a sort of betwixt and between of delicate pink. And so, seated in the casualty ward, he waited for the shouting hordes of the ill and ailing to flock in.

Right in the vanguard of these hordes a problem presented itself. A police officer entered accompanied by two constables in charge of a short, bowed man with sunken cheeks. Placing numerous papers on the doctor's desk, the officer briefly put him in the picture. He informed him that they had raided a hashish den and that everyone had made his escape except for this one man whom they'd managed to arrest. On searching him they had come across a piece of hashish which he had somehow managed to swallow. They had therefore brought him along so that the piece might be retrieved by the judicious use of a stomach pump.

The problem intrigued our friend Abdul Magid: it was one that possessed a certain charm and the solution to it differed from anything else that had come his way so far. He gazed at the handcuffed man standing in front of him and inquired of him in a tone that mingled authority with guile, "Come along—did you swallow it or throw it away?"

The man answered in a tone of utter meekness, prodigious humility, and extreme childlike innocence. "Me, sir? Swallowed what? . . . Honestly, I don't even know what the stuff looks like! By the Prophet, I've been wronged! It's not fair!"

Abdul Magid looked at him: the man had gone up in his estimation. He smiled as though to say, "That's the way, my lad! May God protect you!"

In addition to this silent encouragement, Abdul Magid insisted that the handcuffs be removed. After a short argument, the officer—red-faced, yellow-mustached, and blue-eyed—agreed.

While it is the doctor himself who should undertake the business of the stomach pump, it can in no sense be termed an operation and can easily be carried out by any nurse. The doctor therefore ordered the male nurse Abdul Salam to prepare the solution, and the prisoner—still accompanied by the two policemen—departed to another room, leaving the doctor and the officer alone in the office.

As it was impossible to remain silent for ever, the conversation broke ground on the subject of the girl pictured in the magazine held by the doctor, branched off when the two of them discovering that they had been contemporaries at the same secondary school, that they were both crazy about the songs of Umm Kulthoum, that the officer lived in Abbasiya, where Abdul Magid had a group of friends, and that neither of them had yet taken his holiday because their respective bosses were always giving pressure of work as an excuse for their not being spared. Before the series of discoveries had come to an end the officer said, "My dear fellow, it's really enough to drive you mad! There we were, just settling down to a great session on the roof of a house of someone we know in Heliopolis—a friend of ours had just got back from Palestine absolutely loaded with the stuff. The party was all set, with Umm Kulthoum singing 'The Moonlit Nights Have Come,' and we were just warming up and feeling on top of the world when along comes a detective with a search warrant. What could I do? I had to break away from the party and go off with him. What a bloody life it is! Honestly, isn't it enough to drive you mad?!"

The doctor agreed with him that it was truly maddening, while he gazed at the officer's beautiful eyes, whose blue pupils were foundering in a pool that, though not white, was not yet red but was a sort of betwixt and between of delicate pink. Before he could agree with him further and recount a similar experience that had happened to him one night when he was high, Abdul Salam the nurse entered with a cry of joy, as though he had discovered America.

"Here's the piece, sir. The man brought it up. It's a good two piasters' weight."

"Two piasters' weight?" interposed one of the policemen. "I'll cut off my right arm if it's not a good quarter of an ounce and then some."

"And it's a lovely piece, too—real quality stuff," said the other policeman, with a knowing nod of his head.

The doctor and the officer hurried out of the office and stood either side of the short man, who was lying on a table and emptying his stomach of all its contents, both good and bad. The doctor called out to Abdul Salam to put the piece of hashish, together with everything else brought up by the stomach pump, into a sealed envelope as a court exhibit.

The officer's pink eyes sparkled with joy at having proved the crime and having the evidence safely under seal. Eventually the man was led away, placed once again in handcuffs. As he walked off between his escorts, he could be heard muttering in a weak, agitated voice, "It's not fair. By God, it's not fair."

The Ill-Omened Golden Bird

Ibrahim al-Koni

Abdullah worshiped for four hundred years, then occupied himself with the singing of a bird on a tree in the garden of his house. He was repaid for this by God ceasing to love him.

Farid al-Din al-'Attar al-Nisaburi's
The Conference of the Birds

N
o sooner had it alighted on a scraggy wild bush than, standing bolt upright in front of the tent, she saw the poor child staring at its fabulously bright feathers. Like someone stung, she leapt up and hurled herself at the boy, encircling him with her arms. The tears coursed down from her eyes as she lamented, "No, no, don't look at it like that! It's a delusion. It's a trick. It steals children from their mothers."

But the child was able to detach himself from his mother's embrace with the litheness of a snake and to follow the extraordinary colored bird with the golden wings, the like of which he had never previously seen. He walked toward it fascinated.

The golden bird did not move, did not heed his approach. It waited for him until he was standing in front of it. The child stretched out his hand until it was almost touching the bird's feathers, which glowed under the rays of dusk, then it adroitly flew down and moved a couple of paces beyond the reach of his hand. The mesmerized child advanced farther, almost grasping hold of it. Again it evaded his hand and ran a few more steps. The child was breathless with curiosity and longing, and the extraordinary bird prepared itself for a long chase.

The mother wailed. "Woe is me! Now the chase has begun. Did I not tell you that it is a bird of ill-omen? It lures away children and draws them into the desert. Come back, child! Come back!"

The boy did not come back. He rushed off behind the golden messenger of enticement, which moved coquettishly, flirtatiously, as it made its escape. The child rushed after it, breathing hard, baffled by his desire to grasp it, to take possession of it. On that day his mother rescued him. Running behind them, she caught hold of him and forcibly took him back.

Night fell and darkness reigned. The father returned and she informed him in alarm of what had occurred. He declared with peremptory roughness, "If the bird comes back, shut the boy in. Tie him to a rope and fasten it to that peg."

The bird did not return on the following day, nor for several days after. It then seized the opportunity of the father being away and the mother having gone to visit a friend in the neighboring hamlet, and it advanced upon its confused victim. In the late afternoon it led him on, crossed with him the southern plains, traversing hills and valleys in an astounding chase. The wonderful golden bird would wait proudly until the child reached it and was about to grasp hold of it, when it would slip away, gracefully move off a pace or two, or three at the most, and then stand waiting as it turned to right and left. Sometimes it would direct toward the child an enigmatic look from its small, slyly lustrous eyes and spread its brilliant wings in womanly enticement until the child drew close and was bending over it, certain that this time he would grab hold of it, when it would again slip away with astonishing agility and forge ahead.

The chase continued.

Darkness advanced and finally covered the everlasting desert, and the bird disappeared.

The child found himself soiled with sweat, urine, and fatigue. He collapsed under a bush and fell asleep. At night he was woken by the howling of wolves and heard the conversation of the djinn in the open air. He recited the Chapter of Unity, which he had learned from his mother, as he watched the stars scattered in the darkness of the skies. The stars entertained him with their secret language, speaking to him of things he did not understand. Finally, he became sleepy again.

In the morning, he wandered for a long time in the desolate waste before they found him in a small wadi, lying under a sparse genista shrub with bloodied feet and cracked lips, exhausted and shattered by fatigue.

After the father had forced her to cease her long weeping and she was able to hold back her tears, the mother said that night, "Have you seen what the bird of ill-omen has done to you? It's Satan. Do you not understand?" She shook him violently as, driven by what had happened, she repeated, "It steals children from their mothers. It's Satan—the accursed Satan."

The father stopped her with a brusque movement, and she went back to her sobbing. They were gathered around the stove before repairing to sleep. The boy fell asleep as he sat there.

They had been blessed with him after they had despaired.

They had made the rounds of all the quacks, sorcerers, and

holy men known in the oases of the desert until they had despaired of compassion. Talismans had been of no use, nor had amulets. She had procured the rarest of herbs and people had brought her, from the central parts of the continent, preparations made from snake poisons and the brains of wild beasts.

When they were close to the climacteric, they had been taken to the frightening Magian fortune-teller, who had become famous through dealing with the heathen company of the djinn in the oasis of Adrar.

Had they not sought him out in the plains of faraway Red Hammada he would not have deigned to meet them. The Magian fortune-teller had ceased to receive people and had gone into isolation a long time ago after a continuous series of battles and encounters organized by the Mustansir dervishes against the companies of believing djinn, who had taken possession of the last of the strongholds of wisdom in the desert, claiming that it was armed with talismans and amulets inspired by texts from the Quran. The group announced that the age of idols had come to an end and that the Magian's profession was an abomination, an act of Satan, so he had suffered persecution and was forced to cease practicing his readings that possessed understanding of the darkness and the unknown. He was likewise shunned by people through fear of the violence of the newly converted groups, so the leading pagan fortune-teller found himself isolated and besieged. He sought refuge in a cave in the mountain of Adrar and lived with his followers, in hiding from the arrogant, unbelieving djinn, who vie in breaking open talismans and sometimes in exchanging insulting names among themselves. Often people heard the eminent fortune-teller guffawing in his cave at the jokes of his loyal followers who had applied themselves tirelessly to keeping him amused so as to ease his loneliness.

He received the two of them at the entrance to the desolate

cave that had been hacked out of the mountain top. He addressed them in Hausa. On realizing that they did not understand it, he condescended to talk to them in the Tuareg tongue of Tamahaq. As for the language of the Quran, he uttered not a word of it, and they knew that he was doing this in outrage at the Isawi dervishes, who had swept away his glory in the oasis. His complexion was tanned despite his isolation within the darkness of the cave. He was dressed from tip to toe in black, so that in the darkness he looked like a djinn from the company of unbelievers.

The people of the oasis had come to tremble at his followers, saying that the djinn had become hostile in their behavior ever since the dervishes had entered the Sufi orders and the assemblage of djinn had split into two companies: one that followed the true religion and believed in the dervishes, and one that had remained as they were—unbelieving, idolatrous, and following the fearsome Magian fortune-teller.

Perhaps it was such reports that affected the woman and caused her to tremble at merely seeing this idol sent from the homeland of caves and darkness.

He slaughtered a white chicken at her bare feet and stained her body with blood. He handled her rounded buttocks and toyed with her swelling breasts as he muttered the talismans of ancient idols and tilled her body with his rough fingers daubed with the blood of the snow-white chicken.

The husband followed these rites in a daze. The fortune-teller warned him against uttering any Quranic verses or traditions of the prophets before beginning his pagan recitations in the language of the Hausa and the djinn. He had said, "My helpers do not like that—Quranic verses and biographies of the messengers and prophets are forbidden in my house!"

Then he scattered a powder like incense in the stove. Clouds of evil-smelling vapor rose up. The woman experienced vertigo, while her husband had a sensation of nausea. Then the bronzed Magian again fingered her body, staining it with the remnants of the blood. Finally he said, "We have finished the first stage. Tomorrow you will go with me and I shall show you the tomb in whose presence you must both sleep for three consecutive nights."

After mumbling some cryptic incantations, he concluded by saying, "It is the oldest grave in the desert. It is the oldest grave in the world—the tomb of tombs and the goal of the universe, a goal before people knew of the goal of the dervishes and the beaters on tambourines."

The tomb was a heap of black stones clinging to the foot of the mountain, below the gloomy cave. The first night passed calmly, and the second, and on the third night she saw her shameful dream, which bashfulness prevented her from recounting to her husband. She saw herself being given in marriage to the King of the Djinn. He penetrated her, unusually, in the morning and made her taste such an experience that she still reels at the memory of its frenzy. The frightening king had used her as no human man had ever used a woman. The two of them crossed the vast wadi, making their way on the stones, and she could not free herself of his blazingly feverish body.

She hid the great secret from her husband without knowing that he too had hidden his secret from her, for on that final night she was groaning and twisting and giving vent to her pain from her excessive, agonized pleasure. Neither of them was able to look the other in the eye for the space of several whole months. The fortune-teller had bestowed on them a pagan spell for the await-ed heir apparent and he refused to take payment for his rites.

A few weeks later he saw that she had cravings for certain foods and was devouring white mud.

No sooner was the boy born than she quickly hung the spell round his neck, after securing it in a wrapping of leather and decorating it with magical mosaic colors. When the charm was lost, a year ago on one of their journeys across the desert, the woman was distraught, but the stupid husband calmed her down by saying that he would arrange for her to have a spell from a holy man at the neighboring hamlet, not knowing that the spells of holy men do not replace the charms of the pagan fortune-teller. As soon as the bird of ill-omen came the poor mother remembered her lost charm.

She felt distress and portents of evil.

The golden bird is the messenger of Satan to entice children and steal them away from their mothers. The old women in the desert say that it appears only rarely but when it does, many victims will fall to it, for its appearance is linked to drought and lean years. The old wise women in the deserts of Timbuktu confirm that the secret of its evil omen lies in its golden feathers. Thus, wheresoever the sparkle of the devilish gold flashes, ill-luck makes its appearance, blood flows, and the accursed Satan is at work.

Today the bird has again made its appearance and has lured the wretched boy to his destruction, the mother unaware, for she has gone to the nearby hamlet to borrow a full waterskin.

In the days following its first appearance, precautions were taken. She carried out her husband's order by tying the boy to a peg with rough fiber threads, and she never went out to the pasture or to visit women neighbors in the nearby plains without making sure that the fetters around the bleeding leg of the child were firmly secured. He cried when she was away and would try to escape from the cruel shackle, for the rough rope had carved a bloody collar around his young leg. Secretly at night in her bed, she felt pity for him, but would go back in the morning to secure the rope in her fear for him.

But time is the bane of the memory, the temptation of extinction and forgetfulness. Weeks passed and she grew complacent and relaxed her vigilance. Going away to borrow water, she left the boy loose in the house. The ill-omened bird came after she had gone and abducted the child.

He pursued it in the plains and the wadis; he ascended the heights and went down the hills. The pursuit continued into the late afternoon, and when the time for siesta came the child collapsed, his face set in the dust, panting for breath. The cruel sun was seated on its throne; its rays were released from their hiding-place and burnt the boy with their fire. His tender feet were dyed with blood, his lips were dry, his throat parched of the last drop of saliva.

The bird did not vanish until that moment. It witnessed the shudderings and tremblings of the child, at which it alighted on a wild bush with faded branches and started to spread its fabulous wings and preen them with its amazing beak.

The child regained consciousness before dusk and continued the chase, crawling on hands and knees over the savage stones. He did not turn his gaze to his bleeding limbs and had no sensation of his flesh being lacerated as the stones mangled it, strewing blood on the rocks.

They found the rotting body on the following day under a solitary and desolate lotus tree.

Through the days and nights she wept for him. She mourned him to the desert, the vastness, the wild trees, and the sacred crane. She did not cease moaning until the man took her on a journey to the cave of the fearsome Magian fortune-teller, craving to obtain another boy. There they told her that the detestable fortune-teller had died, and they expressed pride that Adrar had been cleansed for evermore of the filth of idols, but she went to the foot of the mountain where the oldest grave in the world had been erected, and there she lamented as she repeated her misfortune. "Why did You give him to me if You wanted to take him from me? Why?"

The Isawi dervishes answered her question as they swayed ecstatically, beating on tambourines and raising their voices in Sufi panegyrics about divine love, there at the foot of the mountain. "He takes only from those He has liked, and He gives only to those He has loved."

Traveler with Hand Luggage

Naguib Mahfouz

Of an early morning the city appears quiet, clean, almost empty. Its sun, giving out heat, mitigates the winter weather. The family collected itself in the Fiat, the mother driving. He sat alongside her, an item of hand luggage between them. On the back seat were the two boys in school uniform. At his ease, the man looked out at the road.

"How overcrowding takes away from the dignity of the street," he said.

Making no comment, she drove the car at some speed until, a quarter of an hour later, they arrived at the school. The two boys got out and hurried off.

"To the chemist's," muttered the man, and the woman drove to the chemist's, which lay close by on the other side of the road. The man made his way to the shop, bought various medicines for himself and his wife, and returned.

"Please don't forget to take your medicine," he told her, seating himself.

Smiling as she drove off, she said, "To the bank, which is more important."

There was a flurry of movement in the road. It did not start gradually but with the sweeping suddenness of an earthquake: cars, buses, and lorries, all rushing forward as though in a race. The Fiat took a relatively long time to cover the short distance. The man got out and went to the bank, which he found half empty. Drawing out from his account, he stuffed a bundle of notes into his trouser pocket and hurried back. He put the bundle into his wife's handbag with the words, "Spend as much as you need in the time and leave me the rest."

"You're returning tomorrow?"

"Or the day after at the most."

She proceeded toward the station and stopped in front of the east entrance. "Shall I stay with you until the train goes?"

"No," he said quickly. "You've more urgent things to do. Till we meet again, dear."

It pleased him that the station never nodded off: always there was someone going in or coming out—a constant meeting place for those arriving and those departing. Under its high roof, sounds were magnified, echoes reverberated, while from the stationary trains emanated hot, noisy exhalations that triggered the latent beginnings of farewells. Despite being preoccupied with what he had left behind him and with what awaited him there, his heart throbbed. He brought to mind so many journeys, tears, and smiles. Then, with a thought that suddenly struck him, his tongue expressed his inner thoughts: "Glorified is He who possesses permanence."

There advanced toward him a group of passengers, among whom he discerned a woman of mature age who attracted his keen attention. He was intensely startled before he could recover his equilibrium: he was thinking that she had recently passed

24

away. He could not recollect now how it was that this fact had lodged itself in his head. Perhaps it was through some erroneous similarity in names, or some item of news that he had misunderstood.

As she approached him, she in her turn saw him and smiled. Automatically, they shook hands.

"What a pleasant surprise!" he muttered.

"How long has it been? It seems like a lifetime."

They exchanged good wishes, then she went off. His heart beat wildly. He said to himself: If only I were some other man I would have had an affair with her, as in times past. He proceeded on his inevitable way toward the ticket window, from where he went towards the waiting train. A group of people were waiting to see someone off. But what was this?—he knew several of the faces. In fact there was not a strange face among them, all were relatives, neighbors, or colleagues! And here they were, making their way in his direction as though they'd come just to bid him farewell. What was it all about? After all, he would be away only for a day or two, and no one knew he was going on a journey. He was not used to anyone coming to say goodbye even when he went on long journeys. He found himself shaking one hand after another as he said, "What a coincidence that we should all be traveling on the same train!"

"We've come to say goodbye to you!" said more than one voice.

"How did you know I was traveling?" he said in amazement. "I'll only be away for a day."

No one paid attention to what he had said. Surrounding him with evident affection, they wished him a safe journey.

"How extraordinary of you!" he exclaimed with a laugh.

His uncle, the oldest of those there, said to him, "I wish I'd been able to travel with you."

"Thank you. Thank you," he said with intense feeling. "I'm sorry to put you all to this trouble—it's not all that important."

"Why didn't Ameena Hanem come along with you?" asked his maternal aunt.

"I'm going on business and the house can't do without her."

Still astonished, he inquired, "But how did you know of the news, and why have you gone to all this trouble?"

"What a thing to say!" said more than one voice.

The train let out a warning whistle, so he waved them goodbye and went up into the carriage. One of them went with him and put his bag on the rack, while he went down again and stood among them exchanging pleasantries. One by one they left. He closed the door, gave a sigh of satisfaction and seated himself. For the first time he realized he was the only passenger in the whole carriage. How odd! It had never happened before that the train had left without all the seats being occupied. What had happened in the world that he should be taking an empty train—as though he were king of his time! It was certainly a day filled with surprises.

The train moved off. Slowly it glided along, leaving the station and those who had come to say goodbye. It increased speed, the monotonous rhythm sounding unceasingly. He would have time for contemplating and understanding what he had passed through. He sighed and asked himself, "What's the meaning of all this?"

Death of a Dagger

Zakaria Tamer

Khudr Alwan was fed up with his mother telling him fantastic stories about new advances in cosmetic surgery. In a sarcastic voice he asked her, "And do you want to go back to being a young girl of twenty?"

His mother said to him, "Such operations do nothing for people like me, but they are of benefit to people like you. You can now get yourself a new ear in place of the one you cut off in your mad rashness."

Khudr looked at his mother crossly, at which she said to him, "You're now more than forty years old, so are you going to stay a bachelor your whole life? Who will marry you if you stay with just one ear? Every man in our quarter has two ears except for you."

Khudr said with confident pride, "And who told you I'm ashamed of my missing ear and that I don't boast about it?"

"Do you know," said his mother, "that the women of the quarter have forgotten your name and call you 'Lop-Ear'?"

"I'm a man," said Khudr, "and I don't care about what half-brained women say."

Antara ibn Shaddad, the legendary Arab hero who secretly accompanied him night and day, said, "Don't pay any attention to your mother's feeble-minded talk, for though my enemies used to insult me because of my black skin I remained the object of Abla's love and was held in awe by everybody."

"May God be pleased with you, Khudr. You don't understand a mother and a mother's heart. A mother whose son is a monkey sees him as the most beautiful gazelle. I want only the best for you and I see you as the most handsome man in the world, but take a look in the mirror to know that I'm not misleading you. You look awful. You neglect yourself as though you were an orphan; you shave off all the hair from your head and make yourself look bald; you let your mustache grow too large; you don't take care of your clothes, and you've got an ear missing."

"If you let your mother talk," Antara ibn Shaddad told him, "she'll be suggesting that you go to the women's coiffeur to have your hair done."

Khudr looked at his mother. He was sorry for her: she was in her sixties with the wrinkled face of a woman of ninety. She seldom laughed. Giving a sigh, she said, "Make me happy before I die, Khudr. I've become old and am at the edge of the grave, so when shall I become a grandmother and see your children?"

"How extraordinary!" said Khudr. "You have an army of grandchildren. My sister is married and has five little devils."

"But," said the mother, "they are the children of a stranger—they are not your children."

"Today's style is for men to imitate women and women men," Antara ibn Shaddad said to him. "Men have become scarce and their behavior is misunderstood."

The mother was surprised to see her son laughing, whose frowning face only moments before had been almost exploding with rage. In an impatient voice she said, "May God come to your aid with that twisted mind of yours."

Khudr Alwan left the house, after kissing his mother's hand, and went to the Quweiq Lane café. He sat down on his own to smoke a narghile. Antara ibn Shaddad said to him, "Don't smile, for men when they smile too much become like flirtatious women."

So Khudr Alwan's face grew more sullen-looking, and the men sitting at nearby tables became convinced that a stormy dispute was about to erupt. They tried to distance themselves from him, but at that moment two policemen entered the café. One of them shouted a rough order to the customers to get to their feet and raise their arms. They then proceeded to search everybody one by one. On Khudr Alwan they found a dagger with a curved blade. Drawing it out of its scabbard, one of the policemen asked Khudr Alwan disapprovingly, "Don't you know it's forbidden to carry a weapon?"

Khudr Alwan mumbled a few vague incomprehensible words, at which the other policeman gave him a punch. "Don't speak through your nose like that," he told him. "The officer asked you a question, so answer it: Why are you carrying the dagger?"

"Because I like fruit," said Khudr.

"An excuse more vile than the offense."

"The doctor impressed on me," said Khudr, "that I should only eat fruit when it was peeled."

The two policemen laughed. They didn't arrest Khudr Alwan but contented themselves with confiscating the dagger and counseled him to eat fruit with its skin on, so as not to expose himself to trouble in future. Khudr sat in his chair aghast and abashed, as though he had been stripped naked. Antara ibn Shaddad said to him, "He who gives up his dagger is not a man and deserves to sit only among women."

"But it was a policeman who seized my dagger," said Khudr.

"Have you forgotten that policemen are human beings like you and me, that they die just as we do?"

Said Khudr to Antara, "Without a dagger I am weaker than a crippled old woman."

"And how will you get back your dagger?" said Antara.

Khudr sank into dejected thought, then all of a sudden rose from his chair and, almost at a run, left the café. He hurried off to the house of Najeeb al-Baqqar, the man in the quarter with the most wealth and the most influence. He met him and said in a quavering voice, "Listen, Najeeb Bey, all the people of the quarter, great and small, have come to you with demands and I am the only one who has not asked anything of you."

"That's right," said Najeeb, "and it's for that reason I censure you, thinking you don't like me."

"Today I've come to ask something of you," said Khudr, "so don't disappoint me."

"Ask what you want," said Najeeb, "and, God willing, your demand will be instantly granted."

In a choked voice Khudr related what had happened to him with the two policemen and asked him to get back his dagger, considering that the chief of police was his friend and would not refuse him anything. Najeeb thought for a while before saying to Khudr, "Why don't you buy yourself another dagger? I'll make you a present of the best of daggers, one that will cut through rock."

"I'd accept your gift with the greatest pleasure," said Khudr obstinately, "but I'll only be satisfied with my own dagger, which has accompanied me throughout my life."

"This very evening," said Najeeb, "I'll talk to the chief of police and everything will be settled just as you want."

On the morning of the following day Khudr Alwan hurried off to Najeeb al-Baqqar's house and found him still in his nightgown, stretching and yawning. He asked him eagerly, "Everything all right? Put my mind at rest, Bey."

In a voice full of regret Najeeb informed him that one of the policemen, instead of handing in the confiscated dagger to the station, had sold it to some foreign woman tourist and that he did not know either her name or her address. He was going to be severely punished and Najeeb advised Khudr to forget his dagger. "How can I forget it?" Khudr exclaimed. "Do you know that I haven't been parted from that dagger since I was ten years old, that at night I put it under my pillow when I sleep, and that when I go to prison the only thing that upsets me is not having it with me?"

Najeeb said to him, "Make a big thing of it and it becomes big. Make a small thing of it and it becomes small. Even the dearest friend dies, so regard your dagger as a friend who has died."

"I expected to hear such things from everyone else," said Khudr reproachfully, "but I didn't expect them from you, who are the great expert on the characters of men."

Khudr indignantly left the house of Najeeb al-Baqqar and walked through the quarter in an agitated state of mind. It seemed that his dagger was calling to him and he remembered how he used to tremble in rapture whenever he touched its blade and grasped hold of its hilt, convinced that were it to be hurled into the pit of a deep well it would of itself leap up to a mountain top. Antara ibn Shaddad said to him, "Were I to be given the choice between Abla and my sword, I wouldn't hesitate a single instant before choosing my sword, for a man without a weapon is a woman who will not escape being raped."

Khudr Alwan had the sensation of having become without any protection, a defenseless prey, and he yearned for an air different from the one he breathed. He left the quarter and walked slowly along a wide street, on both sides of which stood green trees and tall buildings of white stone. All of a sudden a speeding car ran into him and right over him. He was taken to a nearby hospital but died the following day at dawn. When he was breathing his last, Antara ibn Shaddad said to him, "You have lost nothing, so don't be sad; die unconcerned."

All the men of the Quweiq quarter walked in the funeral procession of Khudr Alwan, and at the head of it was Antara ibn Shaddad with bowed countenance. Khudr Alwan was proud of the fact that Antara had been part of the procession but was sorry that the inhabitants of his quarter did not know that and had not seen Antara piling up the earth with his sword over his dead friend.

Have You Seen Alexandria Station?

Abdou Gubeir

A s they stood under the wooden awning on the platform he said to her, "Do you know"—and she didn't—"some years ago I wrote a story called 'Have You Seen Alexandria Station?'"

She turned with a smile and said, "Really?"

"Yes," he said.

Then he began glancing around at the milling passengers leaving and boarding the trains. But she—because she loved him, and he her, so much so that he would never forget her walking in front of him along the seashore in a bathing costume as he observed her from behind, nor the way she walked afterward in the lights of the city as she shivered with cold, and as he approached her and hugged her to him—because of this, she said, "What's this story about?"

And as he had not in fact written any such story, he said, "It's about two people who are standing on the station platform and talking about their pain, because they're leaving Alexandria and would have liked to stay longer, for they loved the sea, and she

33

liked swimming, though he didn't, because he'd once nearly drowned. But he used to like the way she walked along the seashore beside him, or for them to sit together under the faint light of night and talk as they watched the waves."

"And what about the station?" she said. "Is there a station in this story?"

"Of course there's a station," he said, "because they were standing on the platform and talking about the sea, and about the streets, and about that strange atmosphere that Alexandria leaves in one on leaving it before one's had one's fill of it."

"He definitely loved Alexandria?" she said.

"He loved it all right—and who doesn't love this city?" he said.

"She loves the seashores," she said, "but she's not interested in the city."

"Because she hadn't lived there in winter," he said. "If she had, she would certainly have loved it when she returned."

"Perhaps," she said, "but there must be another reason, because one can't love a city just because it's a city. There must be another reason."

"Naturally, had she wanted to know, there's a love story, but it's between the lines and not easy to make out, because it's extremely complicated."

"Why is it extremely complicated?" she said.

"Because the girl he loved," he said, keeping his eyes on the passengers, "was his wife's sister. He hadn't seen her before, but when he did see her he fell in love with her—and that was of course difficult."

"But why did you make such a hero, someone who seems to love life, who loves the sea, why do you make him have such feelings?"

"He didn't want to and he was sorry about it, but it happened, and there was nothing he could do but record it, which he did."

"Oh," she said.

Then she began to watch the passengers, as he observed her, and they stayed silent for a while, during which she moved restlessly. His wife came back from buying him cigarettes—he was tired and out of sorts and had not been able to go off to buy them himself.

"All you have to do is to read the story and you'll like it," he said to her.

"What story?" interposed the wife.

"The one called 'Have You Seen Alexandria Station?'" he said.

"Did you write a story with that title?" she said.

"Yes," he said. "A long time ago."

"I thought I knew all your stories," she said with a shrug of her shoulders, "but it seems there are stories I don't know of. Are you writing secretly?"

"Yes, sometimes," he said. "But look, the train's coming. Let's go."

But as he was tired and out of sorts, he hung back, as he watched them entering the carriage door. Ill at ease, he cast a final glance at the station, the platform, the people, and that bell.

Women in Fear

Inaam Kachachi

We are seven sisters, all of us frightened. My sister Atika, the eldest of us, was frightened of the cancer that had already devoured her right breast. She had substituted for it a piece of plastic that she used to insert into her bra each morning and that gave her a normal appearance. At night she would put out the light in her bedroom before undressing, then, like someone recoiling from the venom of a scorpion, she would put away the make-believe breast, throwing it into the darkness of the wardrobe and taking care not to glance at it.

Atika lived in constant fear that the cancer would spread to her left breast, her stomach, her throat, her womb, and other parts of her body. She became used to living through the months of anxiety that separated her regular visits to the hospital, though without becoming used to the fear itself.

I would observe the apprehensions of my eldest sister and would enjoy taking her in my arms, stroking her beautiful hair and driving away the specters of fear, wishing that I could do the same thing for my sister Ifaf.

Ifaf is frightened of her husband and the way he continually hurts her feelings, for she had previously been in love with a fellow student at the university, who had then gone off to Holland to pursue his studies and had not returned. Husam, Ifaf's husband, knows the details of her old love story but refuses to let bygones be bygones. No sooner does he have some drink in his stomach than he tortures Ifaf by reminding her of her failed love and of her beloved who had preferred the women of Europe to her.

That daily reminder and his gloating over her misfortune is killing all hope of a harmonious married life. She is frightened of being continually subjected to his insults, fearful that he will drive her to destroy her home with her own hands.

My sister Atifa has no husband to be frightened of. Nevertheless she is frightened of time itself and spends long hours in front of the mirror, touching the tiny wrinkles, pulling at her flaccid neck, putting cream on dry patches, and pulling out any white hairs, without any of it doing any good. In fact, a look of terror springs to her eyes whenever anyone opens the subject of age, so much so that we would purposely ignore any birthday of hers, would not even mention it, lest she fall ill for several days, when all seven of us would fall ill with her.

I used to understand all types of fear, all that is except the one that afflicted my sister Wisal, of her boss at work. It is a feeling that goes beyond the normal awe in which an employee holds those in charge. It is a real fear that makes her pray each day with all sorts of solemn vows for him to be transferred to some other department before he can write a report about her that will lead to her salary being cut, her promotion being blocked, or to her being sacked.

Wisal had joined the Party, though understanding nothing about politics, just so as to appear stronger in front of her boss. But it did her no good and he would continue to watch out for any small slip she might make. His own position in the Party gave him immunity from any prayers or vows of hers, for he would not be sacked, transferred, or pensioned off. She would remain at his mercy, secretly harboring her apprehensions until kingdom come.

Each one of us has her own special fear. My sister Manal is frightened for her fiancé. He is her cousin and it was this young man who had opened her eyes to the fact that she loved him. When they became engaged, Manal was so happy that she became more beautiful, elegant and sparkling. Her fiancé, Nadir, was a recently graduated engineer who was a soldier in the reserve. But the war broke out and instead of Nadir completing his military service in two years it was extended for the duration of the war.

Manal withered. Her sparkle died, her eyes grew dull, and her fear sterilized her emotional feelings. O Lord, don't make of him gun fodder! O Lord, protect him from bombs and shells and spare him from being taken prisoner! O Lord, return him to me safe and sound and take from me whatever You want!

Every time the war entered a fresh year, Manal's fear grew greater, and she became unable to accustom herself to living to danger's rhythm. She would collapse in a fit of trembling and retching whenever she heard of some soldier, the son of a neighbor, meeting his death. She would stay standing on the roof of the house like some wooden doll for a day or two or three just in case there might be some news of her fiancé being still alive.

"O stars, how you look down from your heights at the sorrows of women in fright!" In one of her fits Manal was screaming as she tugged at her hair: "I wish he'd die once and for all so I can be at peace!"

Then she beat her breasts in remorse at the crazy words she had uttered and asked her Lord for forgiveness. Meanwhile, all the efforts of my sister Muna failed to curb her hands and prevent her from injuring herself.

Muna? She is the sister who fears only herself—her headstrong emotions, her fierce outbursts, that fiery, impetuous nature and those prodigious desires, both expressed and unexpressed. She is the most daring of us all, for she fears no one on this earth apart from herself, though she realizes that her daring is leading her step by step to ruin. When we were alone together and were exchanging confidences, I would say to Muna, "I envy you your daring." Then I would knock on wood with a laugh. As for her, she would answer with frightening conviction, "Daring in a woman is a beautiful intimation of a short life."

I am the seventh sister. I used to be frightened of all the things that terrify my sisters, all of them together. I used to be frightened of the disease that lies in wait for me at every breath, and I would be frightened of the years whose days and months turn over more quickly than the leaves of a book. And I used to be frightened of death, which reaps relatives and friends like some voracious hand that plucks people's lives and is never sated. I used to be frightened of my husband, and of his sister, a university professor who did not hide her feelings of discomfort at the fact that I had transmitted to my children the accent of the poor district in which I had grown up.

I was the seventh one in fear. I was in fear of my boss, in fact of all my bosses at work, for my section chief wishes me to be as precise as a computer, while the department chief gives me shameless glances that quickly travel down to my legs whenever I pass in front of him. As for the man in charge of personnel, he never stops inquiring of me about my political leanings and those of the members of my family, right back as far as one can go.

Just as I fear my husband, so am I terrified of the possibility of slipping into the abyss of some casual affair of the heart as an escape from the arid life that surrounds me.

And so it is that I came to fear others as well as myself, and to take refuge in the eyes of my sisters, who share with me the room, the food we eat, and the cover underneath which we sleep, and the overcoats, shoes, and hairpins that we exchange. I would find no lighthouse in their eyes to guide me, but rather echoes of that ghastly fear that dominates us, and so I became more introverted.

Until that day came!

I left home grasping the hand of the girl, together with the two boys, to accompany them to school as usual each morning. It was a Tuesday, a day like any other, in a month like any other, in a year like any other. I would wake up at six-thirty, make the breakfast, wake the little ones, wash their faces while they were still half-asleep, comb their hair and dress them, then put their food into their satchels and hurry off with them to their school before rushing to work.

What devil made me change my routine that day? I told my little ones that they would not be going to school and that I would not be going to work. We would be catching the bus and we would let it take us to the final stop, and meanwhile we would think about how we would spend the rest of the day.

We left the children's satchels with the woman at the top of the street who sold bread. We waited for the bus and squeezed ourselves into it amid the morning rush, slightly disturbed by merely sensing that before us lay a great and different kind of enjoyment.

The bus proceeded sluggishly, like a pregnant woman. Stop after stop it disgorged its contents until we all had places to sit and room for our legs. I exchanged no words with my children, leaving them to their rowdiness and astonishment. I occupied myself with following the ceaseless movement on the sidewalks and asking myself: Among all these, is there a single human being who is wholly without fear? How does a person live who doesn't know fear? How does he walk? How does he talk? How does he laugh? How does he love?

At the final station the driver turned around to us inquiringly. It seems that he had spotted in our eyes that look that cannot be opposed, the look of a drowning man seeking a straw to keep him on the shores of life.

The sun had climbed in the sky and it had become hotter. The driver uttered not a word. He stood up and removed his blue tunic, making do with the short-sleeved cotton garment he was wearing underneath. Then he got down from the bus and removed the sign that indicated its destination, and the number plate, after which he returned to his place, gave a mighty intake of breath and set off with us.

The bus drove through streets I had never seen before. It passed through beautifully clean districts with pretty houses, and buildings that looked like offices in which kindly bosses worked and where women employees moved about at peace.

I did not know that our city concealed all that magic, as it met the rising of the sun's disc and the quickening movement of human life. Baghdad on that Tuesday morning was the warmest of cities, the most tender. How was it that we had not become aware of this ample motherly bosom?

But the bus came to a stop.

What had made the driver put on the brake so suddenly that we were propelled forward in our seats, then abruptly back again? And who was this beautiful girl who had signaled that she wanted to get on?

The automatic door opened and a young woman got in. She looked exactly like my sister Manal. What is my sister doing in this quarter so far away from the family home? Manal got in wearing a red dress, though she had hidden away all her colored dresses ever since her fiancé had gone off to the war. She was laughing away as she kissed me and then the children, telling us that she had decided to join us on this journey which she called "the trip of a lifetime."

Before Manal had settled in her seat, the bus again stopped, this time to allow my sister Atika to get on. She had done her long hair into a plait that hung coquettishly down her back, she who used always to do it in a bun at the back of her head like some old village crone.

Atika looked at us reprovingly as she smiled demurely. "So this is how you two plot behind my back and set off on the trip of a lifetime without me!"

The bus took us along in sprightly fashion as though moving in time with a musical scale that was familiarly chaotic. When it stopped for the third time, Muna got in, without taking the trouble to greet us. She sat down alongside the driver, placing her hand on his as it grasped the steering-wheel, and began singing him a song from an old film.

Then Wisal got in. How had she induced herself to leave her job in the very middle of the week and thus bring down on herself the wrath of her tyrannical boss?

On the outskirts of the city the driver came to a stop in order to pick up Ifaf and her daughter Hiba. She was carrying a suitcase as though going on a journey. She showed no signs of grief at leaving home.

When, finally, my sister Atifa boarded the bus, we all gave a cheer at her radiant smile that made her look ten years younger.

None of us asked where we were going. We were unanimous in disregarding the question, in cahoots with the driver who had descended from the skies. All we wanted was merely to get away, convinced that all directions were equally suitable so long as we were together.

The city was now far away, and the seashore loomed up before us. I had never known before that our city was anywhere near the sea. I did not worry about it. Should I believe the atlas and deny my own eyes?

We went down to the sandy beach, the grown-ups running ahead of the children. Who are the grown-ups? Who the children? What is age? What is life? What is joy? What is fear? What is love? What is freedom? What is madness? Questions that are ruled out in a vast empty space and under a sky open to the impossible.

We ran with our fantasies, racing our shadows until we reached the waves. We were stumbling and laughing and screaming as we experienced the heights of joy. We plunged, together with the driver, into salty depths, washing our eyes with the water of peace of mind, while we freed our skins of the rough, desiccated scales of a lifetime.

Through the exuberance of our bodily and emotional absorption in reaching out to the rare moment, there came to us the sound of Atika singing the praises of life's secret anthem. We turned to her, the sand and salt clinging to our faces, to find that her plait was undone and her hair floating out in all directions as she undid the buttons of her white embroidered blouse, surrendering herself to the sun. We were stunned by the sight. The blouse had exposed two magnificent breasts overflowing with vigor.

We knelt down in the water at the sheer shock of the surprise. That the sea had come to Baghdad was easier to accept than that the extirpated breast had made its way back to my sister Atika's chest. She was dancing across the sands, her hair loose, her blouse undone, like a priestess serving the gods, singing the praises of life's secret anthem.

Did time pass with us as it passes with the rest of humankind in other parts of the world? Had we not agreed that time and all its synonyms were forbidden nouns?

The driver looked at the sun, which had begun to hide itself behind the horizon, and withdrew himself from Muna's embrace, wiping the sand from his head. Then, standing up, he clapped his large hands and said that the time had come to go back.

The new sense of peace that had come over us was strangled merely by hearing the voice ordering us to return. As we tried to protest, our voices blended together with protesting arguments. But he was adamant.

We said to the single Adam in our paradise, "Go away and leave us." He said, "I brought you and I'll take you back." We pleaded with him, bringing forth our most skilled stratagems and employing means of inducement we had not tried before, but he would not change his mind.

He had risen from the sand like some intrepid mythical being. He began stretching out his hands to us so as to draw us away against our will to the bus that crouched over there like some gloomy catafalque. We were not wicked, but the trip of a lifetime cannot come to an end because of the decision of some stranger, even if he be our partner in the miracle. He pulled us by the arms and we slipped away from his grasp. He came at us once more and we banded together against him. He lifted his hand to strike Atifa, so we raised our fists and attacked him.

The sun was completely hidden and a translucent darkness had descended. The seven sisters had regained an integrity of purpose they had lost through remorseless fear.

Muna seized the hand she had covered with kisses and twisted it backward, while Ifaf and Manal rendered powerless the legs of the man who, this extraordinary night, was trying to be an

44

octopus. Though he was strong, we in our madness were stronger. He was a forceful male and we were subjugated females, schooled to fear yet striving for a moment's peace of mind. And so we encircled him with all our strength, each one of us ready to plunge her claws into his eyes, were it not for Atika's voice cutting across us. "Leave the final move to me."

Atika, her hair loosened and exhibiting total well-being after emerging from the siege of illness, with hands washed clean of the clamminess of fear and without the slighest compunction, seized hold of the struggling man's throat. Standing around her, we derived such strength from our weakness that we stifled the breaths that had brought us to the sea of Baghdad lest they take us back again.

An Invitation

Gamal al-Ghitani

H e leaves the small building of the suburban station at the very moment that the electric train moves off southward. The din of the wheels on the rails fades away. Three taxis are waiting as the few passengers move off in the tree-bordered side streets. On the other side is a brightly-lit restaurant, one of a chain that has proliferated during the last few years. But he sees no one inside, neither staff nor customers.

He stops for a few moments before approaching the first car, while taking the envelope from his pocket. He gazes at it for perhaps the hundredth time: the school badge, his full name written out by typewriter. He reads the wording of the invitation to attend the annual meeting of the board of fathers, notifying him of the necessity of attending to participate in the discussion of the agenda and the confirmation of the budget. It bears the headmistress's signature.

Frowning, he tightens his lips.

What headmistress?

What school?

What fathers' board?

He wasn't a father. He wasn't married, and had no children. He was completely on his own except for occasional friends with whom he would meet up casually at the café, and colleagues at work about whom he knew no more than what they disclosed when they chatted. In fact striving to recall their features, he is unable to do so. It doesn't matter, so let him now put his mind to what awaits him. "What children?" he repeats to himself. "How did this occur?" He goes up to the taxi. He only mentions the name of the school to the young driver after the taxi has moved off, at the corner of the square. "Annual meeting?" he asks himself.

The man looks at him in astonishment and says that he's just driven a couple of fathers there already, and adds that he operates only within the suburb, because an officer in the traffic department is going to get him a driving license. If this happens he'll be able to go downtown, and to the airport; the opportunities for picking up fares here are limited and the work is sluggish because most of the people living here are foreigners or wealthy Egyptians, all of whom own not one car but two or three. The station also serves a very poor district whose inhabitants prefer to walk.

There is a complaining tone to what he is saying as he regards the streets that are almost devoid of pedestrians, with trees that are seldom to be seen in such profusion, and walled gardens. He reads a sign written in phosphorescent lettering: "Beware of the Dogs."

The car crosses a single railway line, after which the driver turns right: dense trees, jet-black shadows, high, unkempt weeds. In the dim light emanating from street lamps spaced far apart, he sees an iron gateway. Before he gets out the driver asks him if he knows anyone at the traffic department.

"Traffic department?"

The young man regards him in astonishment.

"I'm a university graduate and I want to work lawfully."

He backs up the taxi more slowly than the emptiness of the street requires. Has he hurt his feelings? He didn't mean to, but his mind is distracted. He is unable to divulge to a soul this strange position he is being forced into.

No sign gives the name of the school. He sees a tall man, dark-complexioned, wearing a sparkling white *gallabiya*, skullcap, and glasses. As he approaches, the man beams at him and grasps his hand in both of his.

"Welcome to the son of goodly folk!"

Does he know him? What's this fulsome greeting about? Having no chance to seek an explanation or ponder it, he smiles shyly. The man raises his finger, calling on the heavens to bear witness that he is a great man, and that if it hadn't been for the contribution with which he had inaugurated the list, the others, with their millions, wouldn't have paid anything. He says that his eye is now much better after having the operation, and that he is able to distinguish colors after a couple of months when he couldn't tell white from black. He says that the man who performed the operation was a student here, and that he had often carried him about on his shoulders and taken care of him until his mother came to collect him in the car. She would be late and the boy would be on his own after the other students had left. He said that he looked out for him—may God grant him success—but he couldn't reduce the bill by a piaster: the hospital is run as a business and must show a profit—even a glass of water was charged for.

"Just imagine it, sir, . . ."

He spreads out his palms as he looks up supplicatingly at the heavens.

48

"May the Lord bless you in your children and bring them success."

Then he turns toward the building, which he has only just seen.

"Go ahead, my good sir—they haven't begun yet."

He is overcome by bashfulness at not being able to reciprocate this Nubian man's fervent affection. Could he have ignored him completely? After all, he hasn't met him before and doesn't recollect ever having seen his features. Yet, even so, the man approached him so amiably.

What is it all about?

He begins to feel fear as it mingles with his perplexity and curiosity. As for the underlying distrust with which he met the envelope when he first received it, there was no longer any trace of it. What awaits him?

At the door of the hall he sees a lady in her forties standing by a high table, on which is an open ledger. She gives a welcoming gesture. Any questioning from him would appear odd now. He remains composed, so as not to express unwarranted surprise, especially when she inquires affectionately about his wife.

At this moment he begins to go along with the situation, though he tells himself that sooner or later he must talk to the headmistress about the strange position he finds himself in. Her surprise will naturally be considerable. He almost laughs at the extraordinary confusion he feels as he answers her and asks after her own health.

From the lady's tone of voice and evident disquiet, he realizes that his non-existent wife is suffering from some illness. Could it be some casual indisposition? Or is it some chronic affliction that keeps her bedridden, news of which has reached the teaching staff?

He makes his way leisurely between the rows of people. The

rear seats are empty. Most of those present are men. Some of them take up postures expressing authority and self-esteem. A few women sit among them. The strong smell of a cigar. He realizes that he is still standing. He tries to elucidate for the first time the situation he is in, the situation of which he is supposed to be a part.

The headmistress raises her head, beckons. Is it to him she is signaling?

He turns around.

There is no one else.

She utters his first name as it is written on the envelope, followed by the title 'Bey,' asking that he come forward to take a seat, and she points to the front rows. She seems insistent. She is singling him out with evident warmth. Cautiously he feels his way to the third seat in the second row. He raises his hand in answer. She exchanges smiles with him. She is seated in the center of a long dais and is wearing a silk blouse with oriental designs and a raised, gold-colored collar. On her head she has a smart silk scarf. She has strong features. Has he seen her before?

To her right is a broad-chested man with a thick head of hair. He is seated in a formal posture. To her left is a tall, thin man with gold-framed spectacles that slide down his nose slightly; they are merely for reading.

His heart gives a tremor of fear: has he made a mistake by remaining silent and not pointing out the error that has occurred? He is faced, though, by something confusing, and a suitable opportunity has not presented itself. Nevertheless, he is fearful that something is about to happen, though he doesn't know just what. It seems that the headmistress had begun her address before he entered the hall and that she had interrupted it in deference to him, for she has gone back to reading from the papers in front of her without any introductory words.

She is talking about a railing that has been put up, about the high number of students in classes, about the contributions in kind that are permitted and others in cash that His Excellency the Minister had not agreed to, about a personal contact that had been made that led to an agreement, about the reduction in school outings owing to conditions being no longer safe, with every now and again a girl disappearing . . . . No, she was fearful for her own children.

She mentions something about the absence of care and the liberal showering of money taking the place of concern and compassion. She makes reference to dangers at the social clubs, with films and drugs and organized crime targeted at boys even in the schools. She refers to what she hoped to achieve and what has in fact been implemented—the extension of courts for tennis and basketball—and to an article in the national press calling for the scout movement to be revived and inviting support. But the most important thing is that the school has been provided with modern computers, the credit for which goes to . . . .

Everyone looks at him. Applause. He is obliged to rise to his feet. Some faces reflect affection, others are reserved. He bows three times and seats himself, after discovering the source of the cigar smoke: first row, fourth seat. The man has his legs stretched out, apparently unconcerned. He blows out the strong-smelling smoke. Why do they allow smoking? Should he protest? Let him wait until he sees what's happening. He is now not only not a father but the author of some enterprise, some achievement of which he knows nothing. He looks at the walls: notices, pictures in which he is unable to make out any figures or details.

The school newsletter is there on the wall. Five names. He is jolted by the second of them: his own name as written on the envelope, linked with a 'Nadia.' So, his daughter's name is Nadia. What does she look like?

He scowls. It is as if he is summoning up ancient hopes that have fallen into oblivion, as though seeing the remnants of some old dream: a daughter who would kiss him before she went to bed, who would rejoice when he came back home, who would ask him, with exuberant curiosity, what he had brought her as a birthday present; a son whom everyone would say strongly resembles him. Sometimes when he calls a friend, he is surprised to hear the voice of the son of sixteen or seventeen so like that of the father. He asks himself, "Is the effect of heredity so great?" The similarity almost verges on congruity.

"Let us begin with the nominations for the Council. The first item on the agenda."

The man sitting to her left moves to the blackboard and writes in chalk: Name of legal guardian. Name of student. Class. Three adjacent columns. The headmistress looks at those present, assigning him an appropriate smile. Hands are raised. Each man rises, faces the others, announces his name and position, and writes on the blackboard his name, the name of the son or daughter, and the child's class.

He withdraws within himself. The men all blend one into another. The cover of the school newsletter, and Nadia—but what class is she in? It seems he has a son or another daughter at a different stage, perhaps preparatory or secondary. What he expected occurs: the headmistress signals to him with a smile. He bows, after having been about to rise to his feet, and spreads out his hand in a gesture above his heart. He says something about giving an opportunity to the other gentlemen.

"But it'll be the first year we'll be without you."

How will things look if she insists and he is forced to stand in front of the blackboard? He doesn't know the names of his children or the classes they are in. He will be exposed—there will be a real scandal.

Her features express sorrow. She motions with her hands: What's to be done if that's what he wants?

The names of the new council are read out. Applause. She announces a scaled-down meeting of the new members. Thus he must wait for her to finish before explaining things to her. He doesn't know what her reactions are likely to be. He is not the person she thinks he is. No doubt there is some startling resemblance to someone else with his features, his attributes, his circumstances. But how had the letter reached him? And this warm reception?

The people begin to leave. Some of them rise to their feet and converse together. He moves to where the wall newspaper is hanging. In the photographs are young girl students aged between ten and twelve. So it's the first stage, the elementary. There are a few lines under each picture. A group of student journalists during a visit to the police station, a group of student journalists in discussion with the head of the society for the preservation of trees.

He looks carefully at the features of the various faces as he wonders which of them bears his name. Where is his supposed daughter?

The short one? The thin one? Or this fat one? One of them bears a resemblance to him: with wide-set eyes, there is something about her, something mysterious that perhaps comes from him, but it's guesswork prompted by the situation.

"Another year gone!"

The man who had been sitting at the headmistress's right says that she was hoping he would serve on the management committee. In previous years he had rendered splendid service that was much appreciated by those in charge. He makes a gesture of thanks and repeats what he said about wanting to give a chance to others. The man points at him.

"But you'll be with us in spirit."

He turns to the pictures

"The fact is that everyone admires the young lady . . . ." He goes on to say that she is courageous, very intelligent, and very good in Arabic. "When she gives the speech in the morning, she doesn't make a single mistake."

"Naturally—" and he points at him. "The son of the swan, as they say, is a swimmer."

So what does he do exactly? When the headmistress talked about the computers, he thought that perhaps he was a specialist in them, that he worked in a large company, or that he was the owner of a concession from such a company. Now the man is alluding to his command of the Arabic language. What, then, is his profession exactly? What does he do for a living? Who is he?

The man says that her brother Magdi is making progress, that he's much better than last year, especially in the two languages, though he needs a bit more self-confidence; if only he had it he would forge ahead like his brother Nader, of whom the school still had pleasant memories.

Magdi. Nader.

To begin with he thought there was just a daughter, but it now appears that he is the father of two sons as well. All the time he is talking, the man is pointing at the photographs. If only he would point at Nadia.

Just so—her name is Nadia. That's how he read the name. If he could only establish which was her picture. How can he ask him about it when he is her father? And what about Magdi and Nader? It would be better to leave before he is exposed, so let him put off meeting the headmistress to another time.

Once again the man is talking about Magdi—it seems he's causing certain difficulties. "Be confident, my dear sir, that we're giving him special attention."

He assures him that he will bear these valuable remarks in mind and that he will give Magdi special attention—"Exactly as you said in your frank remarks."

He makes a gesture of gratitude, and continues giving the smile with which he hides other matters. He makes his way out of the hall. In the spacious courtyard are a number of cars, all modern models. They speed out, one after the other. Inside one of them he spots the cigar-smoker, sitting in the back and talking into a white telephone. But when did these cars come? When he arrived he had seen none of them. He makes his way swiftly to the gate, moving away from the building. A cold wind is blowing and he is not wearing his overcoat, so he is forced to bend into it. How will he get to the station? He doesn't think he'll find a taxi in this area of the suburb. There is no one walking except him. The last of the cars speeds away. He increases his pace, then comes to a stop.

Does he hear clapping?

One of them is making a speech somewhere. The voice approaches, then recedes: a shushing sound like the waves of the sea.

Now he realizes that the distance he has to cover is greater than when he arrived. There is no sign of the gate, of the tall, dignified, dark-complexioned man with the sparkling-white *gallabiya*, the trees planted close together. He clearly hears the applause. He strides on. However large the school, he is bound to reach some part of the road. Should he retrace his steps? What would he then say to the man who clearly appeared to be one of the school administrators? He had a strong desire to know his daughter's picture and her features. The words that were said about her intelligence and personality kindled within him a certain vague sense of pride, as well as a heart-rending sorrow at having missed all that had passed. He stops. The trees

55

and small plants come to an end. He stands at the beginning of a spacious wasteland; there are no buildings, no signs.

Applause. It is distant, very far away. It vanishes. Once again he clutches the envelope, drawing it close to his eyes. He can no longer read the letters because of the sparse light, is no longer capable of retrieving the name that, as it would appear, was congruent with his own.

The Dog

Abd al-Aziz Mishri

bu Salim had a dog. He loved it in the way a breeder loves what he has bred, fed it from his own food, prepared a warm bed for it on winter nights, and did everything possible to protect it from harm.

But a dog must have limits to the way it behaves, limits to the places it goes, the situations when it should bark, and where it puts its tongue.

(And the only good in a dog is what its master teaches it as a puppy. And if it doesn't obey, then it must be curbed, for bad habits take over its natural disposition.)

He entrusted it with guarding the sheep and the courtyard of the house.

A dog has the loyalty of a guard whose watchfulness is not taken unawares by sudden attacks, and Abu Salim came to hold it in affection.

The days flowed by like water irrigating trees. The flock mul-

tiplied and was pleasing to behold; when the sheep were graz-
ing it was the dog that guarded them.

The dog fell ill. Abu Salim gave it the best of things to eat
and drink, but they did nothing to restore it to health. In the
twinkle of an eye it died.

Grief was roused from sleep in the heart of its owner.

He considered that good should be rewarded, so he took up
his trowel and chose, close to the house, a place that dipped
down to the foot of the mountain. There he dug it a grave, then
brought it wrapped up in an old turban and said a prayer over it.

Someone from the village who witnessed this and had a grudge
against Abu Salim reported that he had seen him saying a
prayer for the dog.

And who would accept the testimony of someone who had
said a prayer for a dog?

The sheikh of the village made a great fuss about it: he
foamed at the mouth and the veins of his throat trembled
with rage.

He uttered various invocations and religious formulas, and
cursed the uncleanliness of dogs' tails, and expressed loathing
for the excessive length of their snouts.

He gave it as his opinion that anyone who said prayers over
a dog deserved to be killed.

Fear accompanied sorrow for the lost dog into the heartbeats of
Abu Salim, picking its way through the hairs of his beard that
hung down over his breast pocket. Having thought it over and
made his calculations, he said to the sheikh, "Sir—yes I did do it.
However, the dog, with its last breaths, charged me to make you
a present of ten sheep."

The sheikh's zeal went to pieces. Turning to the left and to the right, he saw a number of people who had come to witness the way he would dispense justice. Then he called to Abu Salim and whispered into his ear that was like a small funnel, "What did you say? How many did the deceased will me?"

A Dash of Light

Ibrahim Aslan

S uddenly, as she sat watching television, Umm Abduh
found the electricity cut off. She got into a panic, for there
was nothing in this world she was so afraid of as darkness.
She rose from the couch and took a step, then came to a stop to
wait for Abu Abduh, who was at Gaber's the grocer. Conscious
of the rustle of his *gallabiya* at the door, she said, "Abu Abduh?"

"Yes," said Abu Abduh and went into the kitchen. She stood
where she was until she heard him rummaging about in the
drawer for the matches, then saw the dim light as he came along
the corridor, and watched the shadow of the towel hanging on
the nail grow larger on the mat and then withdraw to the wall
in front of the kerosene lamp that Abu Abduh was carrying with
both hands. Abu Abduh saw the state his wife was in. He smiled
and placed the lamp on the television, then wiped its glass with
the palm of his hand and turned up the wick. He asked her
where the box of matches was that he had told her to keep so
that she could light the lamp for herself if the electricity went
off. She went back to her place on the couch and said she was

fed up with her daughter Mahasin's children, who never left anything in its proper place.

Abu Abduh listened to her, and took out the screw of paper with the aspirins from the pocket of his *gallabiya* as he stood there, and, placing the two tablets on his tongue, reached for the water pitcher from alongside the television and swallowed them with a drink of water. Then he seated himself on the other couch and stretched out his hand, which held a string of prayer-beads, over his bent knee, while resting his left hand on the cushion. He informed her that Umm Hussein the grocer had given him an old quarter-pound note that morning and that he had now returned it to her son Gaber, and that Gaber had accepted it back from him—and he touched the side of his mouth with the tips of his fingers. Umm Abduh asked him if his tooth was still giving him trouble, to which Abu Abduh said, "Yes."

"Then, dear, have it out."

Abu Abduh shook his head and said, "What's it matter?"

"If it's hurting you."

"Umm Abduh, am I to start having teeth taken out at my time of life?"

Umm Abduh said that everyone had it done at the State Employees' Hospital and that it was better to have some pain for a short time rather than all the time—"Or is there something you have to atone for by going on having trouble with it your whole life?"

"It's not a question of my whole life or anything of the sort— it'll come and go till my time is up."

Umm Abduh thought about her teeth that used to wobble about in her mouth and then fall out without any pain. "I was the one whose teeth gave up on me all on their own," she said. She used to throw them out of the window. "They were perfectly healthy, as good as new . . . . The light's a long time coming on."

61

"It'll come on soon."

"Do you think it's off at the mosque?"

"Yes."

"And at Mahasin's?"

"Maybe it's all right at her place," said Abu Abduh. He said that the children had not put in an appearance, he had not seen a single one of them. But Umm Abduh said that the boy Waleed had been there.

"When?"

"When you were sleeping."

She told him that he had seated himself right down and had said, "Give me a shilling, Granny." He had taken it and, slamming the door behind him, had gone off. Abu Abduh smiled and said that that boy in particular reminded him of Rashid, who used to be in the village. "Remember him, Umm Abduh?"

Umm Abduh settled her body on the couch and said, "Only too well." And she described to him his torn *gallabiya* and his round skull-cap. She said that she used to run after him and tease him—she and the Yahya boys and the Dabbour boys—right from the Tannahi residence up to where he'd disappear from them at Sidi Ali al-Shababi.

Abu Abduh nodded his head and said, "Glory be to God," and he began recounting to her how Rashid used to stand in front of the gate of Sidi Ali and whisper into the keyhole, "Ali lad, peace be upon you. Open up, lad, it's Rashid," at which the gate of the mosque, which was locked with brass bolts from the inside, would open out on both sides and Rashid would go in to sleep and the gate would close behind him.

"He's from the Labboudi family, Abu Abduh."

"I know that—and I know his cousins, every one of them. Their land was on the outer canal."

"What an odd life it is! Do you think Rashid's dead, Abu Abduh?"

"Most likely died ages ago," said Abu Abduh.

Umm Abduh sucked at her empty gums and said, "What a nuisance this business of the light is, I must say. Abu Abduh, when I die I'd like you to wire me up an extension for a bulb in the grave."

"What are you talking about?"

"You know—even if it were just for a week."

It was the first time Abu Abduh had heard any such talk. "It'd blow a fuse, woman."

"Not at all," said Umm Abduh. "By the Prophet, it would be perfectly all right."

Abu Abduh fell silent; it occurred to him that the fuse would not blow. "You're right—what would make it blow a fuse?" Then, thinking about it, his mind drifted to the two Angels of Death and the Reckoning; he asked forgiveness of the Lord and scratched his left leg, and it seemed to him that it would not be possible. He got up from the couch and went into the kitchen and came back with the tea things. Umm Abduh began again to say he could connect up a wire from Abdul Khalik the undertaker and could buy a bulb for a quarter of a pound, together with a socket. "It'd mean the whole thing could never cost more than fifty piasters, even forty . . . . Just for a week, till I got used to the dark."

Abu Abduh placed the sugar in the glasses as he said to himself, "What funny sort of wiring would that be?" He told himself that once he had wired up the grave the wire would have earth tipped over it, and it would then be led under the earth and connected up with the plug the other end at Abdul Khalik the undertaker's. It might be exposed to humidity and someone might tread on it and be electrocuted. "He'd die and there'd be trouble." He lit the spirit lamp and put the teapot on it. He stretched out his hand to her with the matches and asked her not to lose them this time. Umm Abduh took them from him and hid them under the cushion, saying that Mahasin's children were real devils and never left anything in its proper place.

The Cloud

Fuad al-Takarli

I did not ring the bell right away but tried, in the normal manner, to open the door with my own key. This, for no understandable reason, I found impossible. I remained a moment in thought. I found myself rather upset, my brain surrounded by a dark cloud. This was certainly the door of our flat in the fifth sector of the second western district, and I had as usual climbed those six steps, holding onto the iron railing to help my exhausted body on its way up. Then in addition there had passed before my gaze, in their accustomed order, those distorted drawings on the walls and splodges of mud and other filth, which, with the putrid smell of the building, afforded me a black sense of gratification stemming from the knowledge of being in my own place.

There was therefore no reason for the door not to open with my key, for it was the door of my home where I and my family have lived for years without discontent or tedium. Even so, and because every event has something natural behind it that makes it possible within specified limits, and because I had to accept such a proposition, I equally had to accept that I must pursue some other method of entering. I thus pressed the bell.

I was of course tired after hours of continuous work from morning to evening, and I was longing to stretch out in a warm bath to relax, for one's body does not endure the successive harassments of life for long.

After the second ring of the bell, the door slowly opened and I was confronted by Miss Rebab in ornate blue houseclothes. Her face bore signs of astonishment and disapproval, and we remained for some moments exchanging vacuous glances.

"Good evening, Miss Rebab," I said. "You're here, are you?"

With a dexterous movement she arranged her upper garment over her chest, as though finding it more exposed than concealed.

"Good evening."

"Welcome to you!"

I wanted to advance and enter the flat, but Miss Rebab prevented my doing so, pushing the door toward me and exclaiming, "What do you want, Mr. Abdul Kareem? It's not a suitable time for a visit, and I'm on my own."

I stood there, feeling the cloud growing more dense in my head. Since last night it had been settling over me like some wild animal. "What do I want?" My voice was shaking. "I am extremely tired, lady, and I would like to relax at home with my family. Please tell me why you are asking such questions?"

"Your family? What family? You don't live here. What's happened to you? Didn't you move to another flat two years ago?"

"How extraordinary!"

"Please, this is no time for expressing amazement. Goodnight."

She swiftly closed the door, which sent me into a vortex of doubt, forebodings, and other forms of confusion. It occurred to me to ask Miss Rebab, who was in fact the owner of this flat we had rented, for an explanation of her behavior. Had things really occurred of which, in some strange way, I was ignorant? However, I feared her impatience, for she was a spinster of more than thirty, whom one always found in a state of nervous tension for some reason or other. Perhaps she had invented this peculiar excuse to turn me mercilessly away from the abode where I was happy. Yet the proposition of having a discussion with a lady inside her flat—and in her blue nightwear—was a difficult one, whose dimensions could not be precisely taken into account. I therefore turned right around and walked toward the wide window of the courtyard.

I looked down at the distant view of the horizon. Nothing remained of the sun except for a small wick of red light squeezed within a thick black cloud. It seemed there were harbingers of rain on the horizon, making the circumstances of the present increasingly complicated in the short term. To wait in that narrow courtyard, in front of a closed door, with no hope of it being opened, sent a sensation of despondency not only into my depths but also into the atmosphere around me. I was besieged by incertitude, the events of the past occluding from me a clear vision of the future. Again I turned around and sensed that my tiredness would reach alarming proportions if I put off the decision to leave. Miss Rebab appeared sure about a matter that was surrounded by numerous doubts; I thus gave in to an inner prompting that drove me to remove myself temporarily from such people as her, and I began quietly yet resolutely to descend the steps.

I went out into the street, which was already dark in places. I was supposed to be acquainted with it, to know it well, but found that I didn't—I felt as though I had never set foot in it. It is a hateful street that presents no impression of itself, and I loathe it. It's like a person who faces you in suspicious silence, depriving you of both light and air and saying nothing.

I increased my stride. The sources of light were far off and I came to realize that Miss Rebab's words were not wholly correct. I should certainly have had the matter out with her, despite the embarrassing situation—her blue robe and so on. I should for instance have asked her firmly to summon my wife and to inform her that I wished to meet her. Such a simple and straightforward request could not have led to any sort of difficulty. However, I had not done so. Was it my extreme exhaustion or mental lassitude, or the black cloud that was covering my spirit and which then revealed to my tired eyes, unexpectedly, the familiar bus stop that lies by chance close to the big market, so that I am possessed of a feeling of relief? I was certainly walking in the right direction, the direction I had so frequently stumbled along. What good fortune flutters over me this evening! My haste in walking, therefore, was not in vain. As from today I should change my idea that there is no point in working and tiring oneself out, for life sometimes responds, albeit warily, and optimism—despite everything that had happened—would continue to be both profitable and harmless.

I saw her from afar, standing on her own, waiting under the bus shelter. I froze where I was, not believing my eyes. She was in her old blue overcoat with her long, blond hair falling down in a cascade over her shoulders. My heart beat violently as I peered at the slender specter. O God, how my heart beat! Then I advanced toward her. I realized at that moment that good fortune had not deserted me. For no sooner has someone refused to look at me and talk to me than I meet my wife at the very time when I am in the greatest need of her—her of all people. She is the signpost of life, of continuity, and of time to come.

I wanted, with love, to embrace her even before she saw me

and before I greeted her, but I shackled my worn-out self, for such things are to be done in their proper place. I called to her in an ardent tone, "Manal—good evening to you. What are you doing here?"

She turned to me. I didn't understand why it was that I hadn't seen her clearly. I was astonished at the change that had come over her features and the thick glasses she was wearing.

"Can you imagine," I continued, "that I met the owner of our flat, Miss Rebab? She confronted me with her usual boorishness as though she didn't already know me. She didn't invite me into the flat. Imagine!"

Then I began setting forth briefly what had happened to me a short while back. I was astonished that Manal, with a vacuous, misty look, murmured, "Madmen all over the place! God save us!"

Raising her arm, she signaled to a taxi, but the driver did not stop.

"Didn't you notice," I asked her, "that it had a passenger. There was a passenger in the taxi and that's why he didn't stop. Didn't you notice?"

She did not turn around. I was determined not to back off. We were on our own there, at the isolated bus stop.

"Listen, Manal, this is not the place to argue and have a shouting match. Let's go home and calmly and patiently talk things over. Don't you think that's best? I've been tired since last night . . . since last night. O God, how I remember last night! You didn't understand much of what I was saying despite the fact that I was absolutely in the right. I told you not to let me lose my patience.

"I said that, and I went on repeating it. Wasn't I clear? Wasn't I right? And I didn't retreat. You know only too well that he who retreats in a family quarrel loses everything. Aren't I right? And you didn't retreat either. Remember that. I only lost my temper when I was convinced that neither one of us would retreat. And so I lost my temper—and I was right, and I don't want to apologize. That night it was you who began it, and that wasn't nice of you, and it wasn't fair at all. Not at all. I was merely defending myself, my honor, and my very being as a man."

She was gazing at me as she moved slowly backward, in her eye a look of unjustified terror. "Who are you? What do you want? Who are you? What's the matter with you? Who are you? Who are you?"

Then she ran off into the middle of the street with her arm raised as she signaled to a taxi to stop. I was overcome by astonishment as I watched her. The taxi reversed skillfully and came alongside her. Opening the door, she vanished inside. All this took her no more than a few moments. In a state between doubt and certainty I saw the vehicle rushing off at speed before my amazed eyes, then it disappeared into the darkness. I was overwhelmed by a violent longing to join her. I remained standing in an utter daze. How could this happen? I had been able to converse with her for only a few seconds. I had wanted to repair things between us, but she had not let me.

Once again I turned back on myself and began walking with deliberate steps through the darkness. I know that I lied to her when I told her that I remembered all the details of the previous night. I know that only too well. In truth, I did not want to remember anything, not her face, not her voice, nor the picture of her bleeding and battered head as she lay motionless on the ground. I was lying to her—that was all.

The Clock

Khairy Shalaby

I was walking along a dazzling, crowded street—I think it was Soliman Pasha or one like it. I was pushing aside great multitudes of humanity at every step in order to make my way. All the women of Cairo were naked and gave out a smell of kerosene. There were men who looked like gas cylinders licking the backs of the women and placing money between their breasts and their thighs. Suddenly I saw my younger brother in his peasant's *gallabiya* and white skullcap. Shoulders, thighs, and breasts separated me from him. Delighted to see him, I began stretching out my neck so that he might see me.

He too was stretching out his neck. As we drew closer, it seemed as though we would both be going our own ways. However, each of us prepared to greet the other. When I stretched out my hand he did the same by reaching out between the many obstructions. Our hands met in a quick touch that earned us many rebukes and curses.

Then I don't know where he went. I immediately recollected that I hadn't seen him for years. I remembered that I had wanted to ask him about all sorts of things. My question presented itself: Do you know anything yet about our younger brother who didn't come back from the war? But the question did not come out.

All at once I found myself in a funeral procession. I asked who the dead man was and was told it was the husband of my eldest sister, that he had died in the war, and that there had been news of this. I thought those around me walking in the funeral would blame me if they found themselves alone with me, but I didn't know exactly what I was to be blamed for. Then we arrived at a place that I thought was the cemetery. One thing convinced me that I was right—this was the ancient sycamore tree that was in the center of our village cemetery.

While I was standing far off from those who were making their prayers over the body, I saw my younger brother who hadn't yet come back from the war and about whom we had been unable to gather any information, though we had asked everywhere. His long face with its fair complexion was just as I had known it, ever smiling. He was wearing a *gallabiya*, over which he had put on an army belt. I hugged him and wept.

When I told him we'd had a terrible time trying to find out what had happened to him, he laughed as usual and said that we shouldn't have bothered. Then the procession went off again to enter into the cemetery. There was a certain air of reverence enveloping the mourners, although we come from a family scarcely deserving of acts of courtesy. I said to myself, "Such are the funeral processions of righteous martyrs"—and I had a feeling of jealousy for the deceased.

But suddenly I discovered that Dr. Henry Kissinger, President Nixon, and President Ford were walking at the front of the procession and that they were also receiving condolences. The folk from my village had turned out in gallant fashion and were greeting them and smiling just like them. All of a sudden there was no one there at all. I saw nothing in front of me except for a vast expanse of desert that gave off scorching heat and the smell of kerosene. From somewhere came the voice of a reciter chanting the Quran, while the sun, suspended in the sky, was sinking down into the far horizon like a clock without hands or dial.

Fear

Ghalib Halasa

F rom far off she looked to him like a black splodge. It was as he was crossing Kasr al-Nil Bridge in the direction of the Corniche. As he approached, he saw that she was sitting on a stone bench. Her *milaya* was wrapped around her body and over her head, and from the circle of blackness her small face looked as round as a piaster piece.

The young man slackened his pace, waiting to attract her attention. After staring into her eyes he would be able to gauge the extent of her readiness. But she went on gazing into the river and paid him no attention. He hesitated a little, then seated himself alongside her. She gave him a sideways glance, then went back to gazing at the river.

He considered that things were all too clear and that it was up to her to make the next move. But after a while he became convinced that this was quite out of the question and that he could not wait any longer in this scorching heat.

"It's cold," he said.

She turned to him in alarm and astonishment, her eyes wide

and black. The colored part of the eyes was large and attractive, the blackness merging with the honey-colored sparkle. On her forehead were tiny drops of sweat. He tried to say something, but the serious eyes, frighteningly questioning, cut short his frivolous mood. With a sudden movement and a sigh, she half turned her back to him.

On the other side of the river the palm trees lay in an afternoon glow surrounded by a silvery incandescence, the light dissolving in the gaps between the fronds, light of such vigor that it seemed to be gripping them and preventing them from shaking.

He lit a cigarette and began smoking. He decided he would leave once he had finished the cigarette.

The silence between them continued for a while.

"What time is it?" she said, turning to him.

He laughed and looked at his watch. "Why?" he said.

She blushed so much her face became scarlet. "So we know what time it is," she said in confusion.

"And after you know what time it is?"

Her confusion increased. "Just so we know the time," she said.

"It's six o'clock." He fell silent and began looking at the other bank. He told himself that after a while he would light another cigarette and that when he had finished it he would leave.

He thought she had beautiful eyes, yet he wanted to leave the place quickly. He really did want to. After a while she turned to him, just with her face, and said that the heat stifled her, that at home it was hot and airless, while outside it was even hotter though sometimes there was a breeze, and anyway she didn't like getting home too early. She gave a sigh as she rubbed her face with her hands.

When she fell silent the beauty of her mouth with its firm lips became apparent: a mouth for kissing. The conversation between them developed. "Where do you live?" "In Ghouriya," she said. He said he was a university student.

"By the Prophet, may God keep you safe, friend," she said amicably.

She asked him if he was living with his parents and he told her he lived in a flat on his own. She smiled, staring into his eyes with a knowing, insolent look.

Her eyelids fluttered and blood suffused her face.

And she? What did she do? Her husband had died and she had a boy and a girl, and she worked in a factory making nylon bags.

He thought: they all come up with the same old tale.

He did not like listening to the lies of whores. He felt they were making fun of him, belittling his intelligence. He nevertheless felt happy when he found them out. When he saw her sitting on the old-fashioned sofa vainly trying to thrust her feet under it and still wrapped up in her *milaya*, he said to himself, "She's overdoing the role of the innocent young girl." He told her to relax. She lowered her eyelids and said she was relaxed. He reckoned that the final scene in this farce that repeated itself countless times would be for her to put on an act of wanting to leave—"My husband's awfully strict"—and he would press her to stay and she would insist on going and he on her staying. But he would not allow her to play this game: if she told him she had to leave, he would walk to the door, open it, and say to her, "And a very goodbye to you."

She did not say she had to leave but went on gazing around her with amazed eyes.

"Why not take off your *milaya*."

His tone of voice was peremptory and expressed impatience. She loosened the *milaya* and let it fall from her head. Her hair was chestnut-colored, long and with a sheen, the sort of hair one likes to sink one's fingers into and then run them through it to the end. Under the *milaya* could be seen the collar of her dress: a dark red, it was decorated with black circles. He immediately remarked the harmony created by the red color and the ruddiness of her cheeks.

As he approached her he experienced that slight sensation of giddiness that made him incapable of wholly controlling his movements. She turned to him, raising her face and black eyes in which was mingled a grayness that looked like a slight mist hovering over them. He advanced toward her with set face and eyes that glowed feverishly. He came to a stop as he saw the blood drain from her face, her eyes fixed on him, blinking and blinking: a child's face gripped with terror.

He realized that something was happening that he did not understand, something that halted his advance and brought about a feeling of fear. But he was incapable of changing the way he was looking a her.

When she had left he sat on alone. He recalled the gray misty look she had fixed on his face and that cryptic appeal, more like an appeal for help, and he felt he had somehow been cheated, that he had not been sufficiently bold. At the café he was unable to recount what had happened; it seemed to him like something disgraceful, something he had to conceal.

The following day they met on the stone bench. She did not look at him and it did not seem she was aware of his presence. He said to himself, "After all, who is she? I've demeaned myself too much." Yet he did not find the necessary determination to take himself off. He lit another cigarette, while she sat motionless, saying nothing.

When she turned to him he noticed with surprise that her face had undergone an odd change: her cheeks were sunken and there were blue circles under her eyes; her lips were dry. He asked her what was wrong.

Sighing deeply and adjusting the *milaya* around her body, she said, "You know very well."

He told himself that she was having her period, though deep down he was aware of fooling himself. An interval of silence passed, during which he tried to read in her face the true situation.

"What do I know?" he asked after a while.

The blood rushed to her face and she said something he could not make out.

"What do I know?" he asked her again.

She averted her face without replying. Lowering her head, she began looking intently at the river—"Crazy girl, what's she up to?"—and he felt his heartbeats pounding in his head.

Some time passed, during which he followed the movements of a girl who was trying to handle a small boat but could not manage the oars. A young man seated in front of her was giving her instructions. On the prow of the boat was a green paper flag, while on its side was drawn a red eye with inordinately long lashes; underneath the eye was written in bright black lettering: "Zawiya."

The woman turned and faced him. She was angry or sad—he could not make out which. "You don't know!" she said heatedly, looking him straight in the eyes. "You mean you don't know!"

He stopped himself from laughing. The clever man does not laugh in such circumstances. The feeling he had inside him was not one of mockery so much as a rare and delicate one of joy. He would have liked to be able to touch her.

When they were standing in the living room he drew her to him and kissed her on the lips. She was trembling. She placed her head on his shoulder and gave herself over to him. Her body was gently throbbing against his as though it were trying to soothe a child who would not stop crying. Then desire took over. When his embrace of her—an embrace that in any case was not merely that—became forceful, she slipped away from him. She was breathless and her face gave warning of tears.

As such a reaction should only have come from a woman with a social position—a student, a government employee, or a respectable married woman—he was angry and felt insulted. She was, after all, no more than a servant. He seated himself at a distance from her and, without looking at her, asked her to sit down. He lit a cigarette and lowered his head, thinking to himself, "I've demeaned myself."

She sat breathing hard, her _milaya_ wrapped closely around her body and head. His anger was growing: it did not make sense for him to be defeated by her, and were he to be victorious over her, his victory would be of no importance. However, the challenge had been generated within him and, despite all theorizing, it was necessary for him to be victorious.

He smiled at her and said, "If it wouldn't be too much bother, could you make me some tea?"—and he indicated the kitchen.

She went off hurriedly. He thought he would start with her step by step and to hell with being 'clever.' All during this time the throbbing of her body was permeating him.

She came back bearing the tray with a single glass of tea. He asked why she had not put out another glass. She looked at him in confusion and said nothing. He realized he should have asked her to do so.

"All right," he said. "Sit down and you can share my glass."

"Heavens no!" she said. She went back to the kitchen to pour out another glass.

Before she left she leaned over and kissed him on the forehead: it was as though she were kissing a child. Then she said, "Goodbye and keep well,"—and she closed the door behind her.

He woke from sleep after lunch and made his way to the Nile Corniche. He persuaded himself that the whole business was a joke. From the beginning of Kasr al-Nil Bridge his eyes were searching for her. He said to himself, "She must be over there," and he experienced a sensation of loss as his eyes failed to make out that black splodge.

The sight of the empty stone bench was strange and absurd: an error that had to be corrected. The stone bench had become etched in his imagination with her seated on its southerly end wrapped around in her *milaya*, immersed in her thoughts as she gazed at the river. He no longer pictured her in any other way. It appeared as absurd as going back home and finding that the building had disappeared, as though it had never existed.

"She'll come." He was certain she would come. The fear inside him had seeped into every part of his body, had become like ice embedded in his bones. The sun's rays reflecting off the water dazzled his eyes, penetrating them even when they were closed, and this fact was incorporated into the sequence of insults he was enduring. He made up his mind to wait a further quarter of an hour. If she did not come he would leave; he should really leave now because she was not worth bothering about. The sensation of being deserted stifled him: a waif abandoned by the world who yet puts on a bold front.

The quarter of an hour passed. He stood up. Where should he go? It seemed he had no place in the world. He took a few steps, then seated himself on a nearby bench. He persuaded himself that he was no longer waiting for her but just sitting on the Corniche, that his flat was hot and airless, and that here at least a breeze blew from time to time. He recollected with exasperation that these were almost her own words when he had first met her on the nearby bench.

The Corniche began to fill with people out for a stroll. His eyes took in black clothes in every direction, and each time he saw the color his heart pounded. It occurred to him that she might come out, cast a glance from afar at the stone bench, find it empty, and return whence she had come. He thought of going back to the original bench, but his sense of pride forbade that. It was unbearable torture for him, for she might well come and not see him.

Then his heart began to beat with painful intensity directly he saw the woman in her black *milaya*. She was coming toward him. From the first glance he was sure it was not her, yet his excitement increased as she drew near. All at once he believed it was her, and it seemed that if he made the necessary effort, if he did what was required of him—without knowing what it was he was required to do—this woman who was approaching would be, would become Saadiya. All the time he was trying to change, to modify, the lines of that bulky body and sturdy face so that they might be transformed and become Saadiya. The opportunity slipped from him and the woman walked past. A befuddled confusion took hold of him: he must say something to her, must explain to her, prevent her from continuing on her way. She passed by him and he fell into a state of gloom.

His body was perspiring freely. As sensation returned, he rose to his feet and seated himself on the original bench, knowing that he was no longer being 'sophisticated,' that he was demeaning himself. This, though, no longer had any meaning for him. It occurred to him that she might have come and left. How could he free himself from this torture?

The following day he felt he was moving without motivation, without any desire for anything. He was exhausted and restless: lunch, then the afternoon siesta, heavy yet tense. Waking from sleep, he felt a soreness in his throat from too much smoking.

He was both exhausted and tense at the same time.

He made his way to the Corniche with a feeling that there was something he should have done but had not. "Did I leave the water boiling on the stove without turning off the gas? The key, where's the key? Here it is." She was not there. It was as though he had expected it. A frantic, unruly anger took hold of him. "I shall wait for her and take my revenge—I'll give her a lesson she'll not forget." Maybe she has a lover, a mechanic, or a servant in some house, whom she will tell about the young gentleman she made a fool of. She had given him nothing, yet even so, here he was, in the blistering afternoon heat, waiting in vain for her to come. Perhaps the two of them were at this very moment observing him from somewhere and laughing. He saw himself through their eyes: the neck twisting around so as to watch the passers-by, as he moved from one bench to another, the clean ironed shirt, the polished shoes—and he began to feel disgust for his body.

At night, before going to sleep, it occurred to him that perhaps she was ill. The thought saddened him as he brought to mind the picture of her fatigued face with the black circles under the eyes. He felt he should apologize. "I've been unfair to her." As he sank into sleep his hand was gently touching her shoulder as he apologized.

He saw her in a dream. In the first part of the dream she was not there, though she had an urgent, compelling presence. A great number of people were awaiting her appearance. The venue was like a large garden, or an open stretch of land. He tried to ascertain the time but his watch was not on his wrist. He was certain she was late for her appointment with these people.

Instead of electric light there were glaringly bright pressure lamps that gave out a continuous noise. At that instant he remembered that it was said of Lenin that he always arrived at an

appointment on the dot, and did not behave like men of importance who believed they were proving their importance by being
late for their appointments. He did not know where he had read
it or who had said it, though he was certain it was authentic.

Then he saw her pointing her index finger at him. She was
extremely angry and her eyes were very beautiful. She was
speaking excitedly. "You must realize the subtle differences. I
was late because I was tied up with some very important work."

She began talking with the others in a friendly way, though
without losing her seriousness. The subject of the conversation
was the extreme importance of filling one's leisure time in a
fruitful manner. He heard one of them saying that he had to
realize the subtle differences.

During the day he decided to change his routine: lunch at
four instead of two, sleep at five; he would wake up at eight and
thus get through the painful period of the day by sleeping.
What happened instead was that at four he had a feeling of
nausea and a desire to vomit at the mere smell of food. He tried
to sleep but was unable to. At the usual time he was seated on
the stone bench, even more exhausted and even more tena-
ciously expectant. In his trouser pocket he carried a penknife
with a sharp blade.

Seven days elapsed, after which his anxiety began to wane.
Saadiya became, speedily, a mere memory, pleasant and amus-
ing. He might see her one day, and this time he would not be
so weak.

He recovered his sophistication, which he believed he had
lost. He would say to himself, "That madness that came over
me," and he believed it was just something that occurred in the
summer vacation, that slightly perturbed him. He imagined a
sympathetic listener to whom he would give an account—with

certain modifications—of what had happened, an account in which he would appear more in control, more intelligent though no less comical; this was not important, just so long as it was he who was making fun of himself.

Time would ensure that he was persuaded of the veracity of the story in its new version, and yet . . . .

While he was having his afternoon nap, from the first knock at the door, rending the night of his sleep like a rocket, he had known it was her. He rushed out, bathed in sweat, his eyes half-closed, the buttons of his pajama jacket undone. Without checking who it was, he opened the door and hugged her to him. With imploring words he expressed his yearning for her. "What have you been up to? Where were you?" Then: "You beast, my darling, you beast!"

He was kissing the *milaya* that was over her head and hair (why the *milaya* and her hair alone, when the whole of her had been bestowed upon him?).

"The door," she said, indicating the open door.

She seated herself on the chair, her *milaya* still over her head. Then she lowered it, revealing the lines of her body from her breasts down to her feet. He seated himself at her feet and kissed her knee covered by her dress. She drew his head to her breast, encircling him with her arms, and resting her cheek against his hair.

He became immersed in that soft darkness, drugged by its smells, ancient perfumes charged with the association of the incense of the al-Hussein quarter, bringing to mind that dense darkness that surrounded him as he had entered the Qalawun Mosque: the sounds and light cut off and his eyes unable to adjust to the darkness; then, high up in the dome of the eastern corner, he had seen a window made of interjoined pieces of glass, red and green and yellow and blue, pure colors impregnated with the morning sun, and in that instant he was vouchsafed the Sufi's vision: the world of darkness onto which peeps a radiation from Paradise. He was conscious of the fall of her breasts against the sides of his head and on his face, the pressure tightening and relaxing with her breathing. He drank in the smell of her body and its scents, losing himself in that pliant contact, feeling it suffocating and intoxicating as it flowed down in a warm wave to his chest and spread out through his entrails to his loins. An unreasoned desire erupted: to hurt and to devour. Tearing himself away, he spoke in a gruff voice he did not recognize. "I'll take a shower. Make the tea."

He stood under the shower gasping, the tenseness flowing from him. Only then did he become aware of the limits of his body, that he was an entity divorced from the things surrounding him. He walked to the bedroom, the water falling away from his body in a continuous line.

When she left, the flat seemed spacious.

She said she had had a dream. It was then that she had decided to stay away from him, but her heart had not obeyed her. She fell silent. There was something blank and staring and unseeing about the way she looked at him. She sighed and began smoothing her dress.

"May the Lord not let it happen," she said.

Loving that naivety and wishing for more, he told her that everyone dreams, but that did not make them stop seeing one another. Taking her hand, he drew her slowly to him. She said no, where she was concerned it was completely different, for she had dreams that came true. This was something known about her.

She placed her hand on top of her head and began pressing down on it as she said that her hair stood on end whenever she remembered that dream. Then she fell silent. He had become used to this, for she talked only when she wanted to.

Her eyes grew round, the eyeballs widening and, as children do, her lips began shaping the words she was bent on uttering. "In this room." She stopped. Her eyes took in the room. "No, it was larger than this, much larger, and different. Its ceiling must have been of glass because there was sun and pots of greenery and flowers, and when you leaned out of the window you could see the three Pyramids of Giza, blue as if they were made of smoke. It's this room and yet . . . I tell you it was another room, then it became this room. We—you and I—were sitting and talking, and you loved me very much, and you were saying sweet things and I was wonderfully happy, so happy I wanted to cry. Then—wait a little. Then we were in this room. The sofa that's in the living room was here too, and you were still looking into my eyes and saying sweet things to me. Then a strong wind got up, a cold wind with rain, and the sky went black, the whole world was black. You got up and closed the shutters and the windows. You were doing it with difficulty because the wind was pushing against the glass and you were struggling. Then you closed them and the room became black as kohl, so black we could scarcely see one another. I mean, I could see you but not clearly. Then you went to the light switch, and before the room was lit up, you put your head around the door to the living room and you said in a loud, frightened voice, 'Hey! What's up?'

"I heard a faint laugh from outside. I tried to speak, to say something, but my voice failed me. I said to myself, 'It's them, it's them.'"

"Who's them?" he said to her.

"Them," she said immediately, as though it were quite obvious.

"Who's them?" he insisted. "Who are they?"

Her eyes wandered; her mouth searched for words. Turning

to him, she said that it was in the dream. She fell silent as she struggled with herself, then said she did not know who they were, who they could be.

Her body stiffened and she buried her head in his chest and began to tremble. Her breath against his chest stirred up waves of compassion that, if he did not master them, would develop into uncontrollable desire. He began passing his hand over her hair and telling her it was just a dream, that we all dream and that some of our dreams come true, while some are just dreams. Then her body began to tremble with suppressed weeping. He thought the weeping would soothe her.

She left him and returned from the bathroom after a while having washed her face. She sat on the edge of the bed, silent, her eyes lowered. The crying had given her face a delicate softness. Some time went by without her saying anything. Then her body straightened and she gave a deep sigh: it was like a return from somewhere.

"O God, make it all right," she said.

"Yes," he said.

In his attempts to increase his knowledge of her, which up until now had been of no avail, he asked her if she really loved him. She let her head fall onto his chest with passionate impetuosity and encircled him with her arms. This alone was her response.

But why? What was the reason?

He felt her kisses on his chest. He had come to know that to pursue his questions would drive her to tears. This puzzled him greatly, for she hardly knew him and made no attempt to do so, nor did she worry him with her day-to-day problems. Having torn herself away from the fever of bodily contact, she would burst into long, sad monologues about love and dreams and would invariably end up in tears; these, though, did not last long.

She was lying on her back in her slip staring at the ceiling. Her mouth was like a baby's, now round, now distended in her search for words. Suddenly she got to her feet and left the bed for the kitchen, then returned and sat on the edge of the bed. Her palms were spread out on her half-naked thighs. In a daze she pulled down the edge of the slip, staring out with fixed gaze as though preparing to leap up.

As though in recollection, she said, "It was in a long, wide street, with no passers-by or buildings, with flowering trees on both sides. Violet flowers only—the green leaves hadn't sprouted yet. It was dawn and it was foggy and I was walking along that street. I was alone and crying. A car came racing up. I couldn't see it clearly because of the tears and it crashed into me and I died. I shall die like that."

A sensation of disaster was weighing him down. She was revealed to him, lying on the ground, her features set, blood trickling from the corner of her mouth. Two children sat through the night waiting for their mother who never came. He touched her shoulder, then began shaking her and calling to her. "Saadiya! Saadiya!"

Her shoulder muscles were taut and resistant. He felt that she was sitting so stiffly to prevent herself from crying, for suddenly she covered her face with both hands and began sobbing. Her head was bowed, her elbows tucked in at her breasts. Her shoulders shook with eruptions of suppressed weeping. Through her tears she was saying that she knew he should marry the girl who was right for him, but he would go on loving her though he was meant to marry the other one. She would keep away from him, but he would search for her and would not marry the other one. She must therefore sacrifice herself by dying.

He attempted to say something but found nothing to say as she sobbed. He patted her on the shoulder, then began talking to her, saying there was no one else now and that he loved her. He was not able to say anything more.

A rapid series of taps on the door panel. He opened it and she rushed inside; out of breath, she threw herself into his arms, her head on his shoulder, panting and trembling and clinging ever more closely to him. He shut the door of the flat as she held onto him, then led her toward the bed, still breathless. She threw her head back and stared at him. This made him uneasy.

"What is it? What's up?" he said.

"I'm scared, scared to death." She hid her head in his shoulder while her whole being throbbed against him.

"New dreams?" he said, laughing. His laugh was staccato, more like a sob. She replied seriously, saying no, it wasn't dreams, it was a feeling, just a feeling. She grew quiet. He asked her how she was and what she had been doing, knowing she would not answer such questions. She said she would like it if he were young, very young, and she could tie him up in a handkerchief and put him between her breasts, inside her bra, and there he would stay and she would always feel him against her skin.

He moved her away from him. He had the sensation of being smothered. He asked her to make tea. She took hold of his hands, looking at him imploringly, a thin film of tears covering her eyes. "I don't want to die," she said. "I don't want to die."

He gave her a gentle push, saying, "Stop going to those rubbishy films of yours."

She got to her feet.

"Tea," he said.

She brought in the tray with the teapot and two glasses. "You're annoyed with me?" she said as she poured out the tea. Her voice was tremulous.

"No," he said. He spoke it casually so as to stem the torrent of fear.

She placed the glass on the bedside table within his reach and, taking her own glass, seated herself on a chair near the bed.

"Look at me," he said to her.

She looked at him.

"Why are you forever gazing into space?" he said.

She did not reply. The silence continued.

"Why so silent?" he said.

She gave a look of astonishment, then said, "I'm frightened."

He said nothing. He began slowly to drink his tea and lit a cigarette.

"Do you love me?" she said.

He thought: What sort of question is this? Of course he loved her, but he wanted her to stop being so naive. He told her, holding her by the hand so she would listen to what he was saying, "What's this all about?"

He saw her grip tightening on the glass. Her nails had become white. He kissed her on the mouth and said, "Of course I love you."

She plunged into one of her long monologues. Clutching the empty glass, she said, "I tried to forget you and kept away. During that week I tried and tried. During the day I'd say to myself, 'I've forgotten him,' but I'd see a man walking along. I'd gaze at the shoulder blades sticking out from under his shirt, his head turning and observing the passers-by, and I'd be overcome by trembling and I'd say, 'It's him . . . it's him,' and the world would turn around before my eyes and I'd cling to the walls for fear of falling. At night I'd lose myself in fantasies and visions, staying between sleep and wakefulness until dawn broke and the day's movement began."

She stopped, drying her eyes with her sleeve. He felt a shudder pass through his body, a cold current flowing down his spine, for she had delivered her words with the rhythm of female mourners.

Then she went on. "During that week the same thing happened each day, always the very same thing. I'd be sitting in the park near my home, and I'd see you sitting on the stone bench looking at your watch, standing up, then sitting down again, and turning around nervously. You'd move to another bench and sit with your neck twisted around, your eyes peering at the passers-by in search of me. You'd see a woman wearing a *milaya* like mine and you'd be radiant with joy and would hurry to meet her, and your hopes would be dashed. She's not me—and I'd call to you and call to you, 'Do you hear me? I'm calling you, do you hear me?' And I'd plead with you, 'Let me be. Have pity on me,' and I'd see you sitting distracted and not hearing me, and I'd scream and I'd scream and you wouldn't hear me, you didn't want to hear me. I'd tell myself, 'It's your destiny, girl.'"

She fell silent. Her words were jumbled up as she said, "And that penknife you have in your pocket . . ."

Under the surface of intellectualism and sophistication, of a life in which everything is understood and anticipated, there exploded the heritage of far-off centuries of terror. All his defenses had collapsed and he felt himself falling captive to some destiny divinely imposed. With unbounded terror he saw himself the prisoner of some constraining power that would shape his fate, ordaining every step he would take, and however hard he tried to escape he would only sink deeper and deeper into its moving sands.

In the vertigo of panic that enveloped him he tried to cling to the concept of some intricately woven plot: the feigned ingenuousness, the calculated absence for a period of seven days, and his being carefully observed—a plot in which many people participated, very many, and of which he alone was the victim. They had done it to make fun of him and he had unwittingly fallen into the trap.

He said to himself "There are things that are difficult to explain. Coincidences occur. Sometimes the unconscious . . . ." The terror was massive, deep-rooted, and there was no escape from it.

She leaned over him, her breasts weighing down the dress, her face loving and sad. "What is it, my darling?" she said.

She went on giving his hands and hair, his nose and eyes and neck, little kisses, as though she were a butterfly fluttering around his body. He gave himself up to her, totally, pleasurably relaxed. A sense of peace came over him, then desire flared up, sharp as a razor blade, bending his body until it became like a bow. He possessed her eagerly, as though for the first time. During their lovemaking, way back in his head, he observed her frantic reactions, her heavy breathing, as she plunged toward him with voracious frenzy. And there, in some place at the back of his head, lay a question: could it be a plot?

He was sitting on the sofa facing the door of the flat. The lights in the flat were off and the glow from the stairway showed through the door panel. Its thick glass with its smooth protrusions seemed to sparkle like crystal. The lattice-worked frame protecting the glass from outside, with its twists and rounds, traced arabesque lines on the glass of the translucent panel. The flat was spacious and he, in the belly of its darkness, was small and circumscribed.

Her footsteps ascending the stairs were light and hurried. Her feet scraped noisily near the door and came to a stop. He sensed her pressing against the door, resting her weight against it and obscuring the light from a circle in the center of the panel, while the four corners were still lit up.

She gave the glass several light taps with her finger. She moved back and the glass radiated light anew. Exactly in the center of the panel her finger cast its shadow. Then her shadow occupied the whole of the glass square. She resumed her tapping, more urgently and sharply, then waited.

He thought of returning to the bedroom and closing the door on himself and lighting a cigarette. However, he stayed on where he was.

Suddenly her shadow withdrew and the panel cleared, its brilliance hurting his eyes. A heavy silence reigned as though the objects around him were holding their breath. He began to hear the wood of the chair resisting his weight as, ever so slightly, it was being rent apart.

She began hitting out at the ironwork of the protruding panel with the palms of her hands, and the whole door shook. In a choking voice he heard her say, "Open up."

The palm of her hand dwindled, became an almost round fist, then there were two fists. She was striking them hard against the ironwork, whose edges were as sharp as a knife. His body quivered as he imagined her fingers all bloody, the skin detached from the bone underneath. Then, suddenly, she began shaking the door, as she grasped the iron of the panel and shrieked, "Why won't you open, why won't you open?"

She went on shaking the door as she said, "I know you're inside. I can see you."

Then, all of a sudden, she stopped pounding the door and her shadow disappeared. He took a deep breath and cautiously stretched out his legs. He heard the sound of a radio in the distance putting out dance tunes, and drops of water trickling down in a low, regular rhythm from the tap.

Silence, silence, silence as he waited. Her foot scraped against the floor, signaling her presence.

93

Then her shadow filled the glass of the panel. She rapped lightly with her fingers and waited. Then there was silence, as her shadow occluded the light from the panel. Then he heard the sound of her weeping. All of a sudden she grasped the ironwork with both hands and began banging her head against it time after time, as she went on repeating in a weak, weepy voice, "Open up. Open up."

He saw her hands being raised up, and heard the sound of her sobbing distinctly. The shadow slipped away and the panel again admitted the light from the stairs so that he was able to make out her form as she stood there. From the upper floors he heard the voice of a woman calling to the doorman, then the hooting of a car from the street, after which everything was silent. The sound of her footsteps reached him as she crossed the hallway to the stairs, then went down the steps.

Out in the Open

Yusuf Abu Rayya

W hat was I to do? I had eaten a heavy lunch, smoked a couple of pipes of hashish, and had sex with my wife on the double bed—I, the driver of a taxi, in which I tear around amid the fleshy, jostling crowds in streets choked with private cars and buses filled with closely packed bodies.

When the sun casts its rectangle of light on my bed, I rise from sleep to eat a hurried bite, snatch up my sunglasses from the bedside table with its broken flap, and make my way down the staircase with its badly worn steps, shushing away the neighbors' cats busy at the refuse bins on the landing.

I meet the day with a cough that clears my lungs of the remains of the molasses tobacco I use with my hashish, greet the grocer standing behind his counter, say hello to the lad employed at the café on the corner, cross the tramline, and enter the vast garage, from where I set off with my car on my endless rounds.

I am seared by the cold of winter and protect myself against it with a scarf and my old jacket. I am laid low by the heat of summer and seek respite in paper handkerchiefs and flimsy shirts.

What was I to do?

I return every afternoon to find dishes of food discharging their appetizing aromas, to be eaten on the newspaper spread on the floor. I put on my light *gallabiya,* having washed my face under the tap of the bathroom that I share with our good-natured neighbor, his gaunt, skinny wife, and their little devils of children, who hide whenever they see me coming up the stairs in order to jump up and scare me, at which I pretend to be terrified and raise my hands in surrender. They come out from behind the low wall with shrieks of joy at the fright they've given me; I lift a couple of them up, while the third walks along behind me hanging onto my trousers.

I would have liked to have some children like these to meet me on the landing, shouting, "Daddy's home! Daddy's home!" But my wife was always having miscarriages, her womb being too weak to carry the weight of mature fruits. Just once, just the one time in our second year of marriage, she presented us with a boy. Heavens above, he was like one of those angels you hang up around the bed: a full, fresh face, a smooth, white complexion, two tiny, soft hands, and red lips that just asked to be kissed—and he had hardly begun to say "Daddy" when God chose to take him from us. This sudden blow in the face reeled me back, and because it was difficult to leave work to take him to the village where I wanted to bury him with his grandfather, the undertaker lifted him up on his arm and took him off to the Ghafeer burial grounds. Then, at the end of the day, he came to me to say he had buried him there in the tomb of some pasha—yes, by God, a pasha with a great red tarbush painted on the upright tombstone and a piece of marble with his name written in black. I did my duty by reciting the Fatiha and several other verses from the Quran.

When I gave him his fee, he folded it up and raised it to his forehead several times, saying, "They are the dear ones of God. You will find him over there to help you and his mother when you are passing along the Path that divides Heaven from Hell."

What was I to do, you mass of people gathered in the lane, with your eyes staring in at the window to see her nakedness? Could I have just left her in the bath, with soapsuds in her eyes and ears so that she could neither see nor hear? My inner self told me: Better to send her down naked, alive and quaking with terror, than to have the rubble lifted from her shattered body, her limbs scattered about here and there.

And was I ever so selfish as to jump from the window on my own, leaving her there?—she who would greet me on my return home, remove the clothes I'd taken off from the bed and bring me the new clean *gallabiya*, spread out the folded newspaper she'd put aside on the pillow, and place the leftovers from yesterday's meal on it, saying, "I couldn't get any fish. The Co-op's just the end"?

I had returned from the living room drying my face with the towel. We sat down together at the food, as always with the sensation of something being missing, for as we sat there cross-legged we felt the deep desire to fill the void with young children.

Our sole child, before he died, had been able to crawl from his mother's lap and to battle with the spread-out newspaper and stretch out his small hand toward the dishes. We would gently stop him and she would look at me and I at her with joy, for here was our child trying to get at the dish, and we would be stopping him. His mother would calm him down and tear off a small piece of bread and dip it into one of the dishes and put it to his mouth, which he would open reluctantly, as she told him, "Eat up!"

After giving thanks to God and asking Him to allow prosperity to continue, I got up to put a couple of lumps of charcoal on the primus stove and change the water in the narghile. I then opened the piece of red cellophane and cut myself a couple of pieces of hashish to set my blood coursing. I smoked and drank the glass of tea she had made. She asked me for some aspirin, saying, "My head's bursting—the sun was beating down on it for two hours as I was queuing."

I looked in my shirt pocket for an aspirin, which she stirred around with a little tea in the bottom of the glass, after which I closed the shutter of the window that was open onto the bed and leaned back on the pillow to enjoy the gentle light and slight coolness and listen to the blood raging in my veins, until she crept into bed and stretched out alongside me after untying her headscarf and allowing her hair to fall down the sides of her face.

My blood raged still more when I moved my hand to her breast, whose whiteness overflowed her bra. We did as people do, and I went to sleep at peace with myself and with the world. "Praise be to God," I said, and I kissed the back of my hand. "Don't be greedy—tomorrow He'll put things to right."

I was in a deep sleep when I heard the loud crash and the sound of the building collapsing. It was as though the demolition of the world itself had begun, or as though all Hell had broken loose. To start with, I thought the tram had been derailed and was coming through the wall of the house.

But the sound of the stones crashing down at the door of my room told me that what was happening was happening here, in my flat, on the third floor of the old house in Kom al-Shuqafa. I tried to open the door but it opened only a little way, some stones having lodged the other side. I began moving them aside one by one. As the door opened wider I saw that the sky had become the ceiling of the hallway, while the walls of the small room we used for the food safe, the kitchen table, cooking uten-sils, bathtub, and various other things were in the street. Through the space I could see the shops and the advertisements and the buildings opposite and the people pressed together on the pavement looking upward and shouting, "Come down, come down by the window!"

I said to myself, "Where's Saadiya, my wife?"

I heard the sound of the primus stove coming from the bath-room, and saw her hand sticking out from under the door, push-ing aside the stones. At once I opened the door on her, and she screamed as she rubbed the soap from her face. When she saw the void into which I was lifting her, she kicked out with her feet and shouted at the top of her voice, "What a disaster!" I took up the sheet I'd been covering myself with and wrapped it around her naked body. I crawled along on my knees to look down from the window that gave onto the lane and found a fireman climb-ing up a long iron ladder. He saw me and called out, "Come down . . . . Give me your hand."

"I've got my wife," I said.

"Get her out first," he said.

I took up the bashful body wrapped around in the sheet. She was kicking out and crying, and her teeth sank into my shoul-der. Striking me on the chest with both hands, she was scream-ing, "No! No! . . ."

I resented the gawping eyes. When I looked at her, I saw her give a faint smile. I saw the boys jostling each other, on tiptoe the better to see, while I fixed the sheet around her unbridled breasts, her stomach, and thighs, as I stretched out my hands to the fireman so that he might take her from me. Then I began to go down backward, the ends of the *gallabiya* clamped between my teeth, and keeping my gaze firmly averted from the upturned faces.

The Sound of Singing

Salma Matar Seif

"I'll cut your throat, you animal," said my grandfather, "if I see you again with that awful woman."

He was pressing down on my neck with his hulking foot. The harsher his threats against me the more his foot embedded itself in my flesh. Then he moved away, leaving my body like some great throbbing heart. I felt that I was being expanded and contracted, like some desert plant ablaze under the scorching sun.

I approached my heavily breathing mother and looked into her eyes and face. "Does he stop me from seeing her because she's black?"

"Your grandfather, my girl, hates everyone who disobeys him," said my mother. "He has the heart of a pearling ship's captain who coldly buries his divers in the sea's depths. I really doubt his ability to feel the pain you suffer as you lie under his foot. Don't provoke the fury he has for the woman."

I wondered why he prevented me from seeing Dahma, for I had noticed that his state changed as soon as he came to hear that Dahma was living in our vicinity. I found him most of the time grave-faced, staring ahead of him, and eating frugally. Only occasionally would he leave the house. I would see him lying on his side with a glum expression inhabiting the cruel features of his face. At dawn—I had the habit of getting up several times during the night—the sound of his coughing would reach me, together with the smell of the tobacco he smoked in his narghile. I was convinced that something was so upsetting my grandfather that it was making him pallid and ill. This change had come about with the arrival of the woman in our quarter. And when he learned I had visited Dahma, he fell into a rage, exploding in my mother's face and throwing me to the ground and beating me with a severity not used against someone of one's own blood.

I continued paying visits to Dahma, drawn there by my grandfather's hatred for the woman. I was overcome by surprise, for I had seen nothing bad in her to cause me to fear her. In fact, the woman was so beautiful that one was afraid to stare at her for any length of time. She had a physique that was formidable, like that of some mythical goddess, captivating in the way that a fine woman captivates a repressed mortal. The palm of her hand was surprisingly broad, while her head had the roundness of a pigeon's, with facial features that seemed chiseled out of rock.

When I drew close to her I saw her brown neck twisted by cruel blows, as though she had been whipped mercilessly. During my encounter with her, she did not come out of her silence, conversing merely through a wide smile, which she feebly gave from time to time, while I followed her wild look, and I yearned for her to utter. I left her place with a thirst for Dahma, this woman who was tearing my grandfather apart.

"Mother, what's the woman's story?"

My mother, too, was unhappy with me asking about Dahma

and fled from my questioning like someone running away from a blazing fire.

"Mother, I shall go to Dahma and my grandfather can do what he likes about it."

My mother took hold of my hand and I sat down beside her. Her body was shaking as though with a fever. "This woman has a bad reputation, and . . . ."

I went to Dahma. There was an opaqueness about her eyes like cumulus clouds moving in the sky without sending down any rain. I examined her face, her hands, her bosom, and the rest of her body. I did not see it as a body that could lie back and indulge in fornication. I was seeing her in her mythical form, erect like a tree that seeds itself. I feel that my mother's eyes avoid the truth.

"Mother, what's the woman's story?"

My mother's face was afire with cruel yellowness. Swallowing her spittle, she begged me urgently. "Your grandfather will not spare you. Keep away from the woman."

"Mother, I'm going to ask my grandfather about her."

My mother made a moaning noise as she lowered her eyes to the ground. "The woman you're interested in is nothing but an immoral drunk. Look at her eyes."

At dawn, my fear of my grandfather's authority did not check my impulse and I hurried off breathlessly to the woman. I sought asylum with her, my gaze directed at her confused and deranged eyes. I saw the signs of which my mother had spoken: red veins filling the inside of her eye-sockets.

"Grandpa, why do you stop me from seeing Dahma? Is it because she's black? She's beautiful—I've begun to be in love with her."

My grandfather took hold of my hair with both hands, hurting my scalp: it was his sole means of dealing with me.

"You're a disobedient little devil, and I'll break this head of yours. You ask about this whore. Ask, too, about her ten bastard sons."

I waited for the time when my grandfather went out to the gathering of men in the middle of the village souk, and I hurried off to the woman. I don't know the secret of why I lost my mental balance over this woman. My grandfather says she has ten bastard sons. Yet she is a woman on her own, sunk in silence, and around her hovers a secret. It is because of this secret that he beats me cruelly and exposes me to his filthy smell when he is in a rage. And what astonishes me is that my grandfather goes all weak at the mere mention of that woman.

When I went to her I found she was not alone. Beside her was an aged poet whom I know well and see walking along the roads and alleyways, and whose voice I sometimes hear at dawn fervently declaiming. He was sitting beside her, relaxed and happy. I told myself: perhaps this madman is the woman's secret, so I'll ask him. She drew me close to her and I breathed in the smell that emanated from her, like the smell of a date-palm. When I scrutinized her closely, she was not in a position for me to talk to her or to ask the poet for his view. I was tongue-tied and uttered not a word. The poet, too, added nothing. She passed her hand over my chest without making any conversation.

I circled around my mother. With tears I pleaded with her to tell me something about Dahma. She freed herself from me and made off to my grandfather, but he was not there. "She's a crazy woman with no one to tell her how to behave. Her mother was utterly insane and would go out into the highways naked and enter people's houses and refuse to put anything on to cover herself. The people here used to throw stones at her and beat her." At this, my mother stared into my eyes and said, "Then she was found murdered on a rubbish dump." My mother fell silent and I saw in her face a furrow of fear. She turned to me with the look of a wounded animal.

"Why did her mother go mad?"

"The people here were dying of hunger, for the sea was bringing them nothing but tragedy. So they resorted to their black slaves. They all did that, the poor and the great. They began selling them off at the cheapest prices. Dahma's mother heard that her owner was going to sell her, so she shut herself up in her tent and stayed for a whole day seized with fear and anxiety until she went mad."

"Why does my grandfather hate Dahma?"

My mother did not answer. Perhaps Dahma would forever be silent about her mother. Perhaps she was deterred—but by what? I resented my grandfather. I could sleep only for short periods and would sit up the whole night facing a wall that would split open and reveal the face of the woman soiled with silence and an uneasy smile.

Once at dawn Dahma put my head close to her face and there stole upon me a smell similar to that of earth upon which dawn's dew has fallen. "Don't annoy your poor mother," she said to me. "Your grandfather is not kindly."

Then, in the morning, I was standing by my grandfather's head. His features were exactly those of a pearling ship's captain who is practicing his calling by riding into the bodies of pearl-divers, inflating his ego by slaughtering them. But why should the woman be silent, while my grandfather openly flaunts his hatred of her? If he but knew that I cannot bear to be away from her he would strip my body of its heat.

I enjoy being with the woman. She makes me overflow with spiritual ideas that come to those who arrive by the path of the Prophet's Night Journey, while my grandfather wilts with the days at the woman's presence in our quarter.

One night of full moon, the mad poet rapped at my window with his stick and took me out with him to the woman's house. And what a stupendous sight I witnessed: the woman was at the peak of her beauty and vigor, her face filled with a mixture of sternness, a sense of peace, and deep pain. Her eyes had a purity about them that outshone the brilliance of a star or a desert under the umbrella of night. She had lit a fire in the middle of her house and was tirelessly feeding it with pieces of wood. Ouff! What an awesome movement she made as she approached the fire, more like that of a dancer combining joy and sadness, with words and meanings that were halfway between silence and speech.

The poet took me to a distant place. Under the full moon my whole being was replete with an all-encompassing sensation, for Dahma's beauty was oppressing me, was charging me with a burdensome joy and rapturous vision.

"Who is the woman? Why does my grandfather hate her? Is she a whore?"

The poet stroked away my apprehension. "The woman's mother went mad and the village killed her because she went about naked. Dahma stayed on with her master. She was an adolescent girl, and her beauty—as you can see—slays the lecher before the upright. Under cover of darkness he went to her bed, fortified by the fact that he was her legal owner. On the very first night he opened wide her legs and tied them to the foot of the bed. He continued to do so for several nights, bellowing with savage lust. His wife realized what was going on when the girl's stomach began to swell. She became filled with loathing for Dahma. She ordered the girl to hurl herself off some high place to bring about a miscarriage, and herself struck her on the neck and stomach, but the fetus remained in place. Then she put her out of the door."

105

I looked at Dahma. She was still gracefully bending and standing straight as she fed the fire. I saw there was a drum in her hand.

"She stayed alone in a hut of reeds. I brought her food, and after a while she gave birth to her child. Dahma was happy, delighted, dancing with joy. She sang plaintively when suckling the child. One day she stopped me from bringing her food, and she went out to look for work.

"And when one day she came back from work, she found her child had been butchered."

She began to rap lightly on the drum. Soon the sound grew louder, as the fire leapt up like red birds vanishing into space.

"After what happened to her son, I took her in. She was no longer talking and would maintain an awesome silence. Then one morning, she moved her tent right into where people lived in the middle of the village. I only appreciated the significance of this when the men of the village lost control of themselves and roamed around her hut like flies around honey."

Dahma's face was full of the rays of the moon and the night's shadows. She had clasped the drum to the hollow between her breasts as she rapped on it, with her head raised high like an animal when its jugular vein is to be severed.

"The rich went frantic, giving full rein to their base instincts."

"And did she have ten bast–?"

"She would choose the men. If one of them rushed off to her, she would remain with him for several days until she felt that her belly was with child. She would then lock herself up in her tent and keep aloof from men, while the man himself would continue to roam like a dog around the tent.

"And when she gave birth to her child, the reverberating echoes of a penetrating singing were heard in the village; they were heard in the houses and the alleyways and would seep through to the heart of every individual in the village. The sound of singing would continue until the woman had weaned her child, when she would carry him to his father's house. Since the child bore his very features, the father would attempt to conceal those of his own face. The complexion of the child was Dahma's, and the man's will was limp like a wet rag."

The woman began to sing, her voice growing louder, like the voice of a woman in labor.

"She did that with ten men . . . ."

"Then she has ten sons."

"She has dozens of songs that she sings. She does not stop singing, while the village screams. One of the men spoke truthfully about what happened to him with Dahma. He was crying like a child. Dahma, standing like a tree embraced by a desolate night, would cast herself down before him."

"Why does my grandfather hate her?"

"Your grandfather was one of them."

The woman stood upright and sang, and the madman sang with her. I went up close to Dahma. I felt dizzy, with something forming inside me like a ball and striking out in every direction. I clung to the woman and I sang. My grandfather, with his heart of a sea captain, struck out at me as he yelled, "She's insane. I'll flog her till the foreign spirit comes out from inside her. She's insane."

The Charge

Edwar al-Kharrat

I didn't know whom I loved and knew not his name,
and I didn't know who it was I clasped to my bosom.

—Ibn Arabi

awoke on Sunday afternoon.

Was it as if my soul contained the remnants of a sadly evocative song, with someone humming it under these lofty Mamluk domes in the spacious courtyard of some mosque?

The languor of waking from an afternoon nap and the gentle sensation of indolence. Though my room was warm and enclosed, I could feel the summer sea air beating against the glass of the balcony, whose shutters were closed. The late afternoon light drips from its wooden flaps, giving me the impression of a distant sun.

Ambiguous sensations evade me, then slip away. Like my thoughts, fugitive and sly, they are enticing projects that all too soon take me unawares, then sneak off. I listen for them but hear nothing; I stare at them in utter emptiness, grave of heart, pleasurably stimulated by a yearning that is without rhyme or reason.

Here, then, I am returning, wandering aimlessly in futile boredom.

Why all this grumbling? Why am I myself the victim of bewilderment and unspecified anxiety?

It is a melancholy that is indistinct, a depression without a cause, a discontent that wrings my soul. Inside of me is a gloom of misgiving that does not attain to true darkness, nor revert to being light.

Shall I say, "Then is there no way for me to relieve myself of its hardship since it is such a heavy burden?"

Or should I say to myself, as though making fun of myself, "Man, man, death's really lovely . . . ?"

I turn over in my mind plans for the end of the afternoon without as yet moving from under the bedsheet that has become crumpled and is coiled around me: I'll go to the clay pigeon shooting at the Silsila Club and shoot at the pigeons. Or to the Sporting Club, where I'll be in time to watch the final race maybe, or perhaps I'll go for a drink at Athineos on my own. Perhaps there—anywhere—I'll find Antoine or Phillipe Nakhla or Fattouh al-Kaffas? Or I'll go first of all to al-Manshiya al-Sughayyara and maybe I'll take Odette, and perhaps Arlette too, to the six o'clock performance at the Fouad Cinema. What's on? *Marie Chapedelaine.* I hear it's good.

I say to myself, "Shall I visit my relative at her house near Sittat Alley?"

Can she imagine that I'm in love with her? This extremely white woman, with tightly packed flesh, full breasts and skinny legs. She likes to wear sleeveless satin dresses that show off her arms that are like thighs: a joint of veal hung up at the butcher's. But, by the Almighty, she's entertaining, especially when she looks at me stealthily and closes her narrow little eyes in a flirtatious way. Man, shame on you, for God's sake deal gently with the hearts of virgins—and their thighs!

No, I'll go to the Cristal Café after all. Maybe I'll find Abdel Kader Nasrallah there, and I'll play him at backgammon.

Or what shall I do, where to rest my head at the close of this never-ending day?

It is as though my sense of having committed some sin urges me to be on the move in any direction and at the same time prevents me from moving in any direction. And I do not know how the sin can be taken from me.

It is as though my amiability has been interrupted by reason of a scarcity of patience, by feebleness of purpose, indecisiveness, and lack of companionship.

Here I am with my old sheikh Abu'l-'Ala* plaintively droning about my distress in his words: "I bid farewell to my day knowing that one like it, if it comes to one like me, will not return, and that my life is a cloud destined for death, and that my life will unstintingly give itself to death"—or something of the sort.

Odette was at my right while Arlette was sitting to her right, far off in the quiet cave of the cinema in Fouad Street. The small, dim lamps on the plain walls of the auditorium were unostentatious and gave off discreet globules of faintly yellow light that did not prevent me from taking her hand and placing it between mine on my lap. I gently moved her hand little by little until I brought it to my tense erection. She first of all touched it guardedly, then quietly settled down beside it, then eagerly grasped hold of it. By and by she became so excessive with it that she obliged me gently to distance her with the slightest of

---

*Abu'l-'Ala al-Ma'arri, the blind poet, known for his pessimistic outlook on life.

movements to lessen her pressure a little so that the blaze, which was on the verge of exploding, might again become a state of calm incandescence without any impetuous danger. As for Arlette, I was able to make out in the diaphanous darkness her long, soft hair that almost hid the side of her white face, which was immersed in the alternating specters of light and shade.

On leaving, we turned off Nabi Danyal toward al-Attarine. Behind the smartness of the houses and shops illuminated in the summer streets where cars occasionally passed in both directions, lay the small side streets with their low-lying old houses, though the walls, left over from long years ago, looked strong and solid enough. Under them, still urbanely silent and gracious, were the shops of the bookbinders, the wheelwrights, the metalworkers, the sellers of beans and felafel, and the grocers. Here was to be found the odor of serious work, refined service, the fellowship of poverty, respectability, and working into the early hours when required, without any deceit or sharp practice; they still retain pride in workmanship, know-how and the canniness of traditional trades, and the dignity of skilled craftsmen.

In an open, unfenced courtyard, its floor strewn with tamped down sand, in the light of a municipality lamp, the workers were having their supper, the smell of the sea blowing in suddenly from under an ancient tree. The gaslight falls on one side of its vast black trunk, leaving its other half as though chiseled out of pitch blackness, its thick lower branches amputated, with the stumps jutting out from the ancient body. As for the thin, quivering, higher branches that stir alongside the light that permeates them, they are distant garlands of lush, bright green leaves.

They had spread out a copy of *al-Ahram*—in those days the ink didn't smudge—and had put down piles of the broad traditional loaves, piping hot and giving out an appetizing aroma, with wide tin plates filled to the brim with broad beans fried in tomato sauce with cumin and drenched in linseed oil, and radishes with great hairy tops and broad, dark leaves. They were eating with the appetite that comes with being in good company. Without hesitation—and in tones that ranged from the serious to the jovial, between natural generosity of spirit and the required custom of asking someone to share one's meal—they invited us: "Please join us! By the Prophet, by the life of al-Morsi Abu'l-'Abbas. Come along, sir, you and the young ladies—it's what's available. We're serious, sir—this isn't just a 'boatman's invitation.' By the Prophet, the food's really tasty!" I answered, half in jest and half seriously, "Thanks, fellows. May it do you good. May it bring you much health." We went out into Khedive Street and took the clanging, rumbling, and shaking tram, as though we were on an outing, to al-Manshiya al-Sughayyara.

The small army tents were set up in Saad Zaghloul Square, in the garden and directly under the statue. The soldiers were in their round helmets with flat edges, khaki shorts coming well down to the knees, and the dull, yellow puttees wound around their legs. They stood in one short row, with the big gun not far off, its muzzle pointing seaward, and the English Ford lorry laden with a consignment of obviously bored and exhausted soldiers, as the young officer sat on a rush chair in the garden regarding us without interest.

On the same day, 24th July, *al-Baseer* reported: "A woman of Sittat Alley was set on fire and suffered serious burns. She was taken to the State Hospital. Mr. Ismail Fahmi Farag, attorney of the Department of Public Prosecutions, took charge of the investigation. The woman accused one of her neighbors and her two young daughters, O. and A., of collaborating with one of her relatives, a graduate government employee, in setting fire to her. However, the investigation regarded it as likely that the victim had had an affair with her relative the accused and had seen him

112

paying frequent visits to the neighbor and going out with the two girls on several occasions to high-class cinemas. Thinking, therefore, that he was planning to marry one of the girls, she resolved to set fire to herself out of jealousy and to avenge herself on the two girls and their mother. The investigation is still proceeding."

And also: "Thieves broke into the Singer Sewing Machine Company in Sherbeen and stole all the contents of the said place, which is located in front of the police station. On the same day, Persian carpets were being put up for sale in the Nahman shops, the prices starting from 5 pounds, while china plates and bowls decorated with roses were available at the Ghandour stores for 11 piasters, and summer pajamas decorated with braid were on sale for 75 piasters, woolen swimsuits for 28 piasters, and long-sleeved Tricoline shirts for 30 piasters."

The evening show at the Gawzi Cinema in Cairo that night was the social comedy *Road to Safety*, directed by Ibrahim Lama. Walter Pidgeon and Ann Harding were in *Behind the Law* at the Metro Cinema in Alexandria, but I didn't go to see it.

When night falls I am taken over by the usual apprehensions. At such times I listen in the silence of the street to the sounds of car wheels rolling along the asphalt. Are they going on past? Are they stopping in front of the door? I ask myself, "Is that the big van come for me?" The repressed squeal of brakes being applied, it seems to me. I await the thump of heavy boots on the stairs. They are late. They aren't coming. Nothing.

My breathing has quickened. Only now do I realize that my forebodings are crushing me, choking me. I have a sensation of total impotence, of paralysis of the spirit, the extinction of any resolve, and something resembling submission before an inevitable and decreed destiny.

I have pajamas prepared, two clean shirts, two changes of

underwear, and all my shaving things, together with a small mirror, as well as a cake of Lux soap, slippers, toothpaste, and brush. I added a book of English poetry for good measure. They won't, I guess, object to English poetry. I have them packed in a small bag, open and ready. If they come, when they come, at least I am ready for them . . . .

I say to myself, "Haven't the days of secret revolutionary activity passed, with the anticipation of imprisonment or internment? Didn't they pass away long ago?"

I say to myself, "Who knows? Don't the old files still exist, if they were to go to work on them?"

I say to myself, "The story of my relative? Who would imagine it? Fancy setting herself on fire!"

I say to myself, "Yet even if this were so, they wouldn't come, in this sort of a case, in the middle of the night. They'd summons you through an official paper, with a fixed appointment in broad daylight."

I say to myself, "Who knows? Who knows what can happen with them?"

Suddenly I hear footsteps. They come up the stairs, slow and firm. Not many. Listening out for the sound of the car, I had failed to hear it. I listen with a frozen heart. There is not the slightest fear now, merely expectancy.

The footsteps continue upward. They go past my door and die away gradually. I say to myself, "Who would come after two o'clock in the morning?" I say, "Of course, it's my neighbor, my neighbors from upstairs, coming back from a night out, or from being kept late at work, or from some trip. What's strange about that?"

I say to myself, "Why don't the people I'm waiting for go to the ultimate in violence? Why don't they completely encompass the victim? Why aren't they usually like some precise instrument of violence? Is this because of us in particular? With us

114

they go to a prescribed limit, then they come to a stop. Or don't they in fact stop? In al-Ordi, in Abu Zaabal, in al-Mahareeq and the Oases,* didn't it happen?"

I say to myself, "An exception, perhaps a departure from form."

The form is that a moral legacy from childhood intervenes and bars them from going to the extreme.

Or is it that there is an unexpected brotherly affection, bashful and mutual and unadmitted, in the depths of hearts disturbed by the impetuosity of orders?

I say to myself, "I know that when the wheel turns its function is governed by a special law: no sooner do the cogs move than it proceeds to its destination with a rotary power that is irrational and peculiar to itself.

I say to myself, "But halfway along the road, where we are, there is something that shatters this absolutism of mechanics: an old policeman, in return for a couple of honest-to-God piasters or, even more so, for a couple of nice words—the very man who used to employ all his strength when wielding the cane—is the very same man who conveys a letter to your wife—'to the folks,' as I put it to him—or who makes a phone call and tells you what the answer was."

It's true, it's something in the blood with us—and still is.

The alternating sequences of hierarchy, of authority and influence, might bring you down, would in fact do just that so long as the cogs have begun to rotate, right up to the last step of the ladder, until this policeman, or even the most savage of the monsters who sometimes go on and on senselessly beating you, suddenly puts a stop to it, prompted, in all probability, by some obscure moral inhibition.

I say to myself, "Who knows? I might be unconvinced of

---

* *Prisons in which political internees were held.*

anything now, of any faith, in any decisive way. May the Lord protect us."

I again hear the wheels of vehicles in the street and can guess their make, their type and function, their speed, their rhythm, whether bulky or small, until I fall asleep.

Finding myself awake, I breathe deeply: here we are at another day, as though, somehow, nothing is going to happen in daylight. I say to myself, "Is there really a relationship of complicity—or of conspiracy—between the aggressor and his victim in all forms of violence: in words, beatings, in physical or spiritual torture, right through to the sexual? As though it were a relationship of camaraderie between the wild beast and its prey, a common embroilment, as though it entailed a sort of love-making, turned upside down maybe, but none the less there."

Are you, the ravished, capable—be it with your consent or against your will—of making your ravishers—tyrants and murderers—become also your lovers?

With something that is in your soul—or in your soil—you are above oppression, above lust, above death—in fact above the meaning of love and the essence of justice.

What is your eternal, everlasting element that is bodiless and that, even so, is your pure reddish body, your pliable soil, your rough sands, your water, and the vestiges of your rapist lovers?

You, without change, are invulnerable. We love you as you are, as you embrace your Hapi, god of the Nile, who is ever sprouting forth the fertile semen that is squandered; however much he is tamed and held back, he recovers and endows you with renewed life.

I am passing through a small semi-vault hewn out of the friable rocks of al-Dekheila, slightly under the ground. Light filters through to it from wide yet distant openings and I sense the smell of gusts of cold air, as though coming from huge but unseen, wholly silent air-conditioners.

I go down on the rough rock with its surfaces at various levels. I descend gradually, then go up slightly and would slip were it not that my feet inside their shoes retained their grip on the fissured fragments of rocks.

I am treading on one side, avoiding the carcasses of slaughtered livestock. I make out huge camels and delicate goats, as well as calves, skinned and white. I try to bring to mind what they remind me of. I don't succeed. They have stamped on them imprints that are round or hexagonal, recently red on the pericardium of blanched gristle that is slightly lustrous.

I am going down farther and farther. I sense that I am taking refuge in a temporary sanctuary.

It is as if the Bedouin women I left at the entrance to this vault—the cave, the natural basement hewn out of the gray rock—were still standing waiting for me. Broad red belts were wound around their stomachs over their black *gallabiya*s embroidered with meticulous love and decorated with many gold coins that clink and sparkle on their breasts, which I sense to be strong and firm. The rings that pierce their straight noses have serrated edges and the brown lips are tattooed with a dark blue line right in the middle. I say to myself, "What is the flavor of a kiss from those lips?" I say to myself, "I shall never know, though I know its taste and fragrance even now."

The corpse is lying on the ground in front of me. It is covered now.

I remember that I saw the full, white face consumed by fire, the eyes that look at me unseeingly, without a word, bearing an accusation that is irrefutable. The skin that has fallen from her naked back in linear shreds, dead and black, reveals a raw, rosy redness in which are white threads dribbling with pus.

"Is this my doing?" I ask myself.

She is now covered.

And now I am utterly hard-hearted; I feel nothing.

The officer with the gold star on his shoulder, blackly smart in his uniform, writes the official report nonchalantly, bringing the report to a close at the said hour and date, having asked whether I have anything more to add. And so he finishes with the whole business.

Have I finished?

Is there ever a finish? Is there ever salvation?

The boy, alone now, is eating the felafel whose light brown rounds are spread out on a sheet of newspaper, along with a loaf of bread, from the dry blistered crust of which he breaks off one bit after another that has been scorched by the fire under the bulky tree. Only now do I see the tiny green shoots sprouting very close to the ground, from under the knotty protuberances. Do these tender emanations have the promise of a menaced life or will they be quickly trodden underfoot? The windy sea squalls and the smell of iodine, while the cars rush past the edge of the courtyard behind al-Attarine, and the high-pitched bells of the horse carriages ring out.

If he still retained his old feeling of love.

It is still robust and resistant to repletion.

I say to myself, "It's no use."

I say to myself, "Then I shall return to al-Dekheila. Are the Camel Corps camels still standing, craning their long necks downward to quench their thirst from the water that has been newly replenished in the stone troughs?"

The mannequin behind the glass of the shop window in Fouad Street is naked, her joints having distinct minute clefts at the shoulders, above the legs, in the middle of the waist, at the meeting of the thighs, and at the base of the hands, which she stretches upward in a wooden movement of enticement with steady gaze; her dull blond hair is dead, without any sparkle; the mount of Venus is flat, dammed in utter barrenness.

She is screaming.

A continuously piercing scream emanating from indescribable pain.

No one hears. No one heeds.

My love is eternal, enduring.

The policemen come, dressed in black, asking about me, pointing their rifles at me, with fixed bayonets, naked and perforated at the tip, tapered and with sharp blades. They walk up to me with firm, resolute stride, their heads inclined forward.

The bayonet thrust penetrates, hot and without the least pain.

The little stone of my heart is not broken.

The charge stands; it does not go away.

Apples
of Paradise

Brahim Dargouthi

D on't concern yourselves with me overmuch, for I am a woman who has had more than what I'm entitled to. I lived for forty years after my husband's death. I awaited death's knife and bared my jugular vein to it without fear or dread. I have said to Azrael on cold winter's nights as I laid my head on my arm, "When you set foot in my room, don't tread on tiptoe, for I am not afraid of you. Set in motion a bell above your head or let off a bomb. I want to see you when you seize hold of my soul and put it in a small cage and fly off with it to I know not where. I want to see that small sparrow that they say comes from my nose as I depart this life."

Then I cover myself up and go to sleep.

I have stayed waiting and baring my jugular vein every night. Yet he hasn't come.

I told you not to concern yourselves with me overmuch, friends, for it is not worth your while following my story. Thus, basically, I recount it to myself. Only to myself. Perhaps 'Mr. Know-All' will tell you words that are nearer to the truth than what I have said. That is up to you, for I shall not judge you and shall not ask of you to take my side. I merely hope you won't say that I'm a feeble-minded woman, for, by God, I am unjustly treated and do not deserve all the suffering that my son and my daughter-in-law Munjiya have heaped upon me.

Do not call me a mad old woman before listening to the whole story, then be fair to me in respect of my son and call down mercy upon me, may God have mercy upon you.

A Gazelle in the Trap

When my mother Maryam gets angry with me, she curses the moment I sprouted inside of her. She used to do that when I was young; when I grew up she stopped cursing me openly but perhaps continued to do so inwardly.

Once when I asked her about my father she said, "Your father died before leaving you a picture of him in your memory."

He left me on my own and went his way.

My mother Maryam used to go to the markets at a time when a woman who looked out from behind the door would have her throat cut. She bought cheap pieces of cloth and would trade with them, selling them to women inside their houses.

"I swear to you, by the Omnipotent Lord, that this is a piece of Indian silk."

"But its price is very dear, Maryam."

"Take it and pay for it by installments."

"No, I can't do that, even by installments, for you know how stingy my husband is."

My mother would say to her, "Don't worry—I'll fix it."

I knew what she meant by "I'll fix it," but that used not to concern me greatly. I would go to Uncle al-Jilani and say to him, "My mother says the gazelle has fallen into the trap. Our appointment is for tonight after the evening prayer, in the paddock of Beni Kilab." Uncle al-Jilani pays the woman the price of the cloth and the woman pays it to my mother and my mother pays me the price of some Syrian halva. Once again she goes off on her own to the souk, the men's souk, and she buys some bottles of cheap perfume, incense and paper screws of nuts, chewing gum and sticks for cleaning the teeth. She knocks at doors and the veiled women open up to my mother and trade with her for goods with "I'll fix it." Uncle al-Jilani isn't stingy with his money, and I enjoy myself with Syrian halva. This went on until I reached the age of manhood, when she ceased to entrust me with conveying the news of the gazelle who had fallen into the trap to Uncle al-Jilani for passing on to the men who paid and went to the paddocks after the evening prayer.

Maryam Restores Virginity

"How much will you pay, O mother of the bride?"

"A hundred francs, Auntie."

"A hundred in advance and a hundred when the guns boom out."

I take the hundred and shove it in the box and ask the visitor to return at night with her daughter.

How lovely she is! She's worth her weight in gold!

I open her legs for her and put the middle finger into the opening and measure it. "Who deflowered you, my girl?"

Her cheeks redden and she cries, "I beg you to keep my secret, Auntie. My father's no longer alive and the man promised to marry me and he broke his promise."

I move my finger about in the wide opening, "Why did you let him do these things to you?"

"He promised to marry me, Auntie."

Her mother hits her on her mouth, her face, her stomach, and tears out some of her hair and wails, "You've ruined your life, you good-for-nothing. Tongues will be wagging about you."

She pictures to herself the scene in the lanes of the village: her daughter riding on a donkey, her face spattered with black and the children screaming behind her and the women throwing stones at her from behind doors until at evening she reaches the house she left to the sound of drums and pipes.

"Have pity on me, Mother Maryam. Guard my secret, don't give away my condition."

"Don't be afraid, my girl—I'll fix it."

I bid her farewell with her mother and go off on my own to bring the medicine for maidens whose virginity has been taken. Then I enter with her into her new home and I sit down on the rug. We look at the bridegroom who's being made a fool of— poor fellow! Generally he is more frightened than the girl. I let out a trilling cry of joy as he steps across the threshold, and another one when, as agreed, the bride lets out a cry when the bogus blood flows down between her thighs, and yet another trilling cry of joy as he throws us the "gown of chastity" and the women gathered in front of the door begin to dance. They grab hold of the gown drenched in blood and dance in the courtyard of the house, and the bride's mother cries with joy and guns boom out from the rooftops. I take hold of the other hundred francs and shove them into the box.

Live Coals in My Pants

We were young. At night we'd collect in an open space in the middle of the street. We'd get some firewood and make a fire, a large one, and we'd dance around it and sing. Then when the flames had died down we'd gather around in a circle, boys and girls. Ezzeddin would tell us stories about ghouls and the sons of sultans, and about weddings that went on for seven days and seven nights. Aisha would go into a dark corner and Yasmeena would join her there and prepare her for the bridegroom. She'd comb her hair and plait her pigtail and spread under her a heap of earth. I would join them there to sleep with her. Yasmeena would open my trouser button and I'd lie on top of Aisha on the heap of earth and Yasmeena would look at us and let out trilling cries of joy and would smack me on the bottom, and she would call out to Ezzeddin for him to sleep with the bride. Ezzeddin would still be telling stories about ghouls—"And had not your welcome preceded your words, I would have eaten up your flesh together with your bones!"—and about the sultan's son who was still looking for "the fragrant apple" that restores youth to an old man. Aisha refuses to sleep with Ezzeddin and Yasmeena threatens to give us away. The young bride gives in to the lying threat of the girl, and Ezzeddin lies on top of her so that she can smack him on his bottom. Aisha's mother arrives, blows on the fire, and takes up a large live coal to put inside my trousers and burn my flesh. "Please forgive me, Auntie," I say to her, "I shan't sleep with your daughter again!" She forbids her daughter to play with us and Yasmeena complains to her mother, who threatens that she'll tell her father. She cries and says to her, "Speak to Mother Maryam to look around for a husband for me! Everyone of my age has married and I only find children to play at bride and groom with." We children grow up and we can't get hold of women. In the brothels they want payment in advance, which we can't manage, so we have to look around for stray female donkeys with which to have sex!

No, Not Now, Azrael!
They told me that my son had married a she-donkey; so, at my wit's end, I bought him a wife and asked him to fill the house with boys and girls.

The first girl came, then the second, and so on until the fifth, and not a single boy survived. When the first boy came he died of measles. As for the second one, he died of a flux of the stomach. The girls came and they filled the courtyard of the house. Their mother was like a locust. By the time the boy finally came I hated life: I had reached the stage where I couldn't stand up or collect my wits together. I had been looking forward to rejoicing at a circumcision party the like of which the village had never seen. But it came when I was baring my neck to Azrael every night.

His mother had given presents to all the women of the village on the occasion of circumcision celebrations: eggs and milk, tea and sugar, and lots of money. Every night she would calculate how much money she had coming to her from the women, and what she would purchase with these dirhams when she came to lay her hands on them on the day of the circumcision. She was dreaming of gold around her neck and on her hands, of the color television, the fridge, and the electric fan she would be buying by installments.

But Azrael, whom I'd waited for all this long time, didn't come. He came only when I didn't want him! He came the night of the child's circumcision and took possession of my soul. I saw him taking out the small sparrow from my nose and about to place it in the cage. I asked him to delay it for a day and a night, just for twenty-four hours. I said to him, "The body doesn't matter. Take my soul but leave the cage hanging from the ceiling. I want to see how the family will mourn me." I embarrassed him when I kissed his hand and wept like a mother bereaved of her child, so he agreed to return the following day.

My daughter-in-law Munjiya came in to see how the joints of lamb in the large pot in a corner of the house were doing. Then it occurred to her to talk to me. She called to me but I didn't answer her—of course not, for I was dead. She placed her hand on my forehead, which she found to be cold. She saw my staring eyes, my rigid body. She wrung her hands, scratched her cheeks and bit her fingers. I was happy. "The poor thing," I told myself, "is going to weep tears at my death." Then I hear her saying, "The bitch! She couldn't find any other time to die! What shall I do? I'm ruined and have lost my money. Everything I gave to the women on the occasions of the circumcision of their sons is lost. You're ruined, Munjiya, ruined by that bitch!"

My body grew even more rigid as I heard her. My soul was frightened and clung closer to the bars of the cage. The same thoughts came to me as when I was in the transient world. The whore! The daughter of a whore! You woman who had lost your virginity! I restored it for her with my own hands and married her to my son! I shielded her from scandal, telling myself it was better for him to marry her than running after stray she-asses! I repaired things for her more than the once after evenings in the paddock, and I didn't say a word to that idiot son of mine. I know that most of the daughters are hers alone and that my son played no part in producing them. I clothed her and clothed her whelps from the money of the men who paid up after the evening prayer. And here she is now all distressed because I've died before she was able to collect back the whoring monies I'd earned all these past years and distributed to the rest of the harlots as presents for the circumcision of their sons!"

She began wandering around the house not knowing what to do. The loud sounds of the drums and the pipes came to her, and the drumming of the dancing women's feet on the ground agitated her, increasing her fury.

She crouched above me, telling herself that perhaps I was having a nap. She called to me in brassy tones, then shook me violently by the shoulder until my head banged against the dirt floor. When she was sure I was dead she wagged her middle finger in my face and said, "Confound you, you old woman! I shan't spoil my son's festivities for a monkey that's going to hell!" Then she shut the door of the house behind her and went off to join the great circle of dancers.

Apples of Paradise

I learned of my mother's death only at night. When I asked Munjiya to give me my supper she said, "Your mother has died."

"What?" I said. "My mother's died! When?"

"At midday," she answered.

"Why didn't you tell me?" I said.

"Do you want me to spoil things for my son because of the death of your mother!" I couldn't believe her.

I went to her house. I saw her lying on her back, her eyes open. I called to her, "Mother! Mother!" She didn't answer my call. I went down on my knees and placed my ear over her chest to hear the sound of her heartbeats, but I heard nothing. I raised her hand and let it fall, and it fell back like a piece of wood. I crouched down like a dog that's been beaten and my heart blew up until it became like a wet ball, and I burst into tears. I cried as I did when, for the first time, I saw a man greedily taking his fill of her! I called to her and wept. I struck out at the man crouched on top of her and wept. I sank my teeth into his shoulder as I wept. He screamed, rose to his feet, and began kicking me. I fell against my mother's outspread thighs. She quickly got up and pushed the man out of the house, then came back to me. "Why are you crying, now?" she said. "Be quiet—I've turned the man out." But I went on crying, both awake and in my dreams. I continued to have spells of weeping whenever I saw my mother's friend entering our house, right up until the time he bought my silence one night with a toy train.

As I grew up I would leave the house and meet up with Aisha

and Ezzeddin, who told us stories about the sultan's son and the fragrant apple and the ghoul who was never satisfied however much human flesh he ate. Aisha would undo my trouser buttons and say, "Leave Ali the sultan's son looking for the apple, for here on my breast are all the apples you could want!" So I would eat the apples and drink pure milk and honey and would stamp on the viper's head and refuse to humble myself. And I'd eat again the apples from Aisha's bosom. I would drink mellowed wine from Aisha's mouth and have no shame about my private parts, becoming boisterously drunk as I danced with her, while Ali, the sultan's son, went on roaming about in the deserts and saying hello to the ghouls—his greetings always preceding what he had to say! Why, mother, do you die now? Why ? Why? And what shall I do with the Quranic injunction that one should not say harsh words to one's parents and with the Prophet's saying that paradise is at the feet of mothers? And Uncle al-Jilani, will he enter Paradise? I don't know what to do.

But the solution has come to me! I shall go out to them all: the men and the women, the dancing women and the drunken men, with my wife among them. I'll say to them, "Good people, may your joy be everlasting. We who have extended the invitation thank you for coming. Now goodbye to you. Give our regards to your families. Leave us—and thanks!"

But the drunken men may become troublesome and the women dancers may refuse to leave the dancing area, and my wife will be displeased at my interference in her affairs. So what shall I do?

Or shall I ask them politely, talk to my wife on her own, and say to her, "My mother has died, dear wife of mine. By the Almighty, she's dead, so don't make a worse scandal for me in the village!" Yes, I know she's stupid and stubborn and doesn't easily understand anything, and that she's a bitch, the daughter of a thousand dogs, so what shall I do if she refuses to go along with me?

Shall I complain about her to the police?

But the police will say it's a family matter and has nothing to do with them.

Yes, by God—I'll complain about her to her mother. But her mother hates my mother and will agree with her daughter that we'll lose all the dirhams we've paid in the past to the village women if the celebration is turned into a funeral.

Why didn't the idea occur to me before? Just to say to the revelers, "My mother's died. Goodbye!"

But the wretched woman might tell the people I was drunk and didn't know what I was saying, and order me to be shut up in one of the houses.

"What shall I do, mother? Tell me what to do, I'm really at a loss."

When I raised my head toward the ceiling I saw a cage hanging there. Inside the cage was a small bird, the like of which I had never seen. I stood up and stretched out my hand to take it, but it was no longer there! I again sat down on the floor and the door opened and Uncle al-Jilani entered—Uncle al-Jilani who had died long ago. He was just as I'd known him before: tall and broad, with a beard dyed red with henna. He came closer to me, and with every step my life was reduced by ten years until I had become a child playing with a train. He patted my hair and said to me, "Get up, boy! Go and play with your friends in the street." I put the train under my arm and went out. When I turned around I saw him stretching out his hand to the cage hanging from the ceiling and taking from it the bird whose like I'd never seen. Taking it in his hand, he pressed it into my mother's nose as he kissed her. I slammed the door behind me and found my wife right there in front of me.

"What shall we do now with your mother?" she said to me.

When I didn't reply she went on: "You'll say nothing until we've finished the celebration—it's winter and her body won't decompose!"

"When will you finish collecting the money from the women?"

"Tomorrow morning," she said.

"I'll go tonight and dig the grave. I'll dig it by myself."

I went to the cemetery.

I dug a grave for my mother.

And another grave for the train.

And in a third grave I buried my clothes

And wandered off into the open country—naked.

Corncobs

Salwa Bakr

S eated in her shack, she gazed out at the piece of land that ran centrally down the length of the street. Her constant apprehensions took her thoughts far off to where her husband, full nine months ago, had gone to that faraway city to work with a contractor. He had not returned and the little money he had left with her was almost exhausted.

With a sigh she again made a solemn pledge to Him who was in the heavens that she would buy bones for a whole fifty piasters for the dog to eat its fill if He who was seated in the uppermost heaven granted her His protection and saved her from the shame of having to beg by bringing back the breadwinner once again to his young children.

She contemplated the stretch of land well covered with rich alluvial mud in preparation for sowing with seed to become a garden to decorate the broad street. Despite the passage of numerous years it had not been cultivated by anyone, and no one had gone anywhere near it apart from a group of people living in the nearby buildings, who sometimes scooped some of its earth into pots to grow flowers on their balconies.

She felt for the cloth bag hanging around her neck and lying between her breasts in which she kept her money. It contained the ten pounds that was all that remained of the money left by her absent husband. She came to a swift decision: she would take the risk and buy a measure of corn seed to sow in the rich soil and try her luck.

Zarifa had already thought of other possible solutions to extricate herself from her difficulties, such as going off with her children to join her man in the city where he was working. But would that not be a truly hazardous undertaking? It was quite likely that he had died during the time he had been working there, as happened to many others. In that case, what would she do with her children in a place where she knew no one and no one knew her?

Once she had had the idea of collecting up her children and making her way back to her village. But what sort of life would she have in that village after having tasted city life? To sleep on the pavement was a thousand times better than stretching out in that wretched mud hut in which she had been born and had lived for so many years. The accident that had happened to her youngest daughter had underlined for her what it meant to live in the city. The little girl had been playing with some children by some sewerage pipes piled up near her shack; a steel pipe had fallen on the little girl and had severed two of her fingers. Zarifa had rushed her off to the general hospital, where they had saved her life. If this had happened in the village she might have died before she could have been given first aid, with the nearest hospital some four hours from the village.

A mere two months later, Zarifa found herself sitting by the highway opposite the general bus station grilling her first crop of corncobs and selling them to passers-by.

The employees at the municipality were not concerned about what Zarifa had done with the government's land they were in charge of, for they had not put a foot on it since spreading it with alluvial mud some five years previously, thus deluding the local inhabitants into thinking that the government was about to cultivate it with a view to beautifying the street. The employees had then placed the amount allocated to planting trees and grass on deposit at the bank and at the end of the year divided among themselves the accrued interest, though without touching the original sum. In this way they ran no risk of being brought to account in this world by some busybody in authority who might one day think of asking them about it; nor did they run any risk of being brought to account in the afterlife, the interest being regarded as a boon that had somehow descended upon them from above, God having inspired one of them with the idea of putting the money on deposit.

A budding journalist lived in the district and used to take the bus to her work from the stop opposite the field of maize. She spotted Zarifa and the smoke from the roasting corncobs and the husks strewn about and decided to write something about the phenomenon of the increase in vendors of roast corncobs, which she would include in her illustrated article about pollution that she had just about completed.

As for the teacher at the local school for the blind, he became a hardened addict of corncobs, thus guaranteeing her a regular daily income of twenty-five piasters, this being the price of the cob he ate while waiting for the bus after his day's teaching.

This discerning teacher had discovered that a corncob was the best and cheapest method of silencing the chirruping birds in his stomach at the end of the morning's work, quite apart from the fact that it was delicious and nourishing. It replaced the two half rounds of beans and felafel, together with a small bag of pickles to speed them on their way from throat to stomach, that cost exactly sixty piasters. It also spared him the early morning quarrel with his wife, who constantly refused to prepare him something to eat, arguing that she had no time at that hour of the morning, as she too had to get to her job on time.

A watchman for what, in governmental parlance, was termed 'pipes and sanitary drainage equipment,' or 'sewerage' in the parlance of ordinary folk, was one of those who benefited from Zarifa's project, for no sooner did he get a whiff of the roasted corncobs, wafted by the breeze to where he sat or slept during his shift of guarding the pipes, than he would get to his feet and make his way with solemn steps to the owner of the business. He would then turn over the cobs in his search for the largest and freshest. Zarifa, though, would spare him the embarrassment of showing preference for any particular one by herself tearing off the green covering from the largest one to hand; then, having quickly roasted it, she would pass it to him in exchange for no more than fifteen piasters, which is to say at a discount of around fifty percent, this in conformity with the facilities normally offered by the state to those employed in the police force.

The correspondent of a famous American magazine was on his way to visit an Egyptian girlfriend who worked on a local English-language paper and used to help him with his work, besides assisting him in solving his sexual problems. Spotting Zarifa, he drove his car toward her. He began taking pictures of her, photographing the world of roasted corn on the cob, to add to his reportage about the city of Cairo, one of a series under the title "How Do the Inhabitants of the Third World Feed Themselves?" While researching the series he had met up with a car auctioneer, match and pin vendors, jugglers, beggars with monkeys and others with Quranic verses, vendors of lupine seeds for nibbling, and vendors of jasmine—all of whom were to be found standing with their wares on the banks of the Nile.

When Zarifa noticed that the man was taking pictures of her, she became furious, presuming that the government was keeping an eye on her in readiness for doing her some harm. This sprang from her deep belief that the government would only come anywhere near her if it had something bad in mind. What reinforced Zarifa's suspicions were the journalist's black hair and somewhat coarse features, his father having been of North African origin.

Nevertheless, she resolved to deal with the government in a conciliatory manner. Hurrying along to the man, she forced a smile onto her face and said, "Have I done anyone any harm? Have I done something wrong?"

The man did not reply, for he had not understood a word. Instead, he put his hand into his pocket and handed her a whole five pounds. Zarifa could not believe her eyes. She asked God to give him victory over his enemies and expressed the wish that the Almighty would protect him in all his comings and goings. She then left him and went back to her corncob activities, while the American continued to take pictures of her. In the meantime her children occupied themselves with tearing the husks off the corncobs and playing with their emaciated dog, which had long been exposed to the unsuccessful assassination attempts of the police squad specializing in stray dogs. The last attempt had been two nights ago when the children had received an urgent warning from the policeman guarding the sewage pipes that the squad in question was about to launch an offensive in the district. The children had at once searched around for the dog and shut it up in the shack with strict instructions not to open its stupid mouth.

Despite Zarifa's good gains from selling corncobs during the summer months, dark clouds were gathering and she found herself wondering what she would do with her life once winter came with its cold and its stormy gales. There would then be fewer people walking about the streets and the children, having gone back to school, would stop buying corncobs. She wanted to find an alternative source of income to provide for herself and her children every day. As for her big dream, it was that life might one day smile on her and make it possible for her to buy a pair of gold earrings for her youngest child instead of the two twists of thread that hung down from her ears. But it seemed to Zarifa that this dream would never be fulfilled, that she would for ever be eating her heart out. She was particularly fond of the youngest girl, though her husband had no love for her and had doubts about her being the product of his own loins. Zarifa was aware that these doubts of his were only too well-founded, for the girl's beautiful features bore no relation to those of either Zarifa or her husband. What made her so positive about this was that the girl did not bear the basic hereditary characteristic shared by all her brothers and sisters and which had been inherited from their father, that small bony protuberance growing at the bottom of the spine just where the buttocks begin.

But God alone knew that it was by sheer chance that the girl happened to be illegitimate. What had occurred was that Zarifa had been with her husband and children in a remote region of the desert, the husband having been transferred to work on digging an underpass. They were all living in one of the tents of a large workers' camp when, early one morning, she had discovered that the man who had slept with her that night and was lying beside her fast asleep was not her husband. She had let out a scream that woke up her husband, who had been sprawled out on the sands the whole night, having gone out to sleep in the cool air. In alarm he had jumped to his feet in response to her cry, together with several men and women occupying nearby tents.

After investigating the incident, the workmen had held an impromptu trial of the persons involved. On being questioned, Zarifa had stated that the man had not had intercourse with her by criminal force and that she had in no way felt him to be a stranger. He had followed the procedure normally adopted by her husband: he had given her a prod in the thigh, had then grasped hold of her breast, after which he had stripped her naked and laid down on top of her until he had had his fill, in exactly the same way as her husband did. She herself had been half asleep, as she generally was in such situations. As for the man, he had sworn by everything sacred that he had lost his way back to his tent, which he had left in order to go outside in the dark to relieve himself, and that after entering the tent and having intercourse with Zarifa, he had gone off to sleep again. He had not had the slighest suspicion that she was not his wife, for she was, in this matter, no different from his actual wife.

Both the moon and the traditional trial by fire known as _bashaa_ had testified to the man's innocence, for he had taken the test of licking the brass drinking vessel, brought to red heat, without his tongue being burnt, which showed that he had not been lying. Also, all the witnesses confirmed that the moon had not appeared on that particular night. Thus the court held that the incident was one of fate and divine decree, though it none the less fined the accused a couple of pounds, the money to be paid to Zarifa's husband in compensation for the wound to his honor.

Zarifa's husband had time and time again expressed his doubts about being the father of the girl when she had been born approximately nine months after the incident. Zarifa, however, continued to assure him that the girl was his, though knowing that she was lying. The only thing that concerned her was that it was she who had given birth to the girl and that she had descended from her womb, and it was for this reason that she loved her and wanted to buy her a pair of gold earrings that could be sold when the time came for the girl to be married, so that an appropriate trousseau could be bought. Zarifa had more than once admitted to herself her worry that when her husband returned he would do to the girl what men so often do, considering the two small buds that had sprouted on her chest and the fact that her thighs had filled out by virtue of all the corncobs she had consumed.

Despite the difficulty she was in, Zarifa rejected the idea of cooking *baleela*, that dish of boiled wheat and sugar, and selling it through the winter instead of roasting corncobs. It would require a large investment in sugar and wheat and a copper cooking pot, besides the great quantity of kerosene required for cooking the wheat properly, in addition to the number of plastic tumblers and spoons, and the screen to protect the fire from being blown out by the winter winds. The project seemed to her to be as unrealistic as the government's birth control schemes.

Even to work at cleaning flats in the district was no longer a possibility, after many of those for whom she worked before had discovered the disastrous mistakes that had resulted from her poor sight. The final straw was when Zarifa had replaced the picture of one woman's mother-in-law upside down. The lady in the picture was seated, dignified and sedate, in a chair upholstered in red velvet; the picture was in an expensive gilt frame and had been draped with a black silk ribbon after her death three weeks previously. When the husband had returned home to find his mother upside down in her chair, he had had a violent quarrel with his wife, accusing her of showing contempt for his unfortunate mother even after her death and of trying to make fun of her before even the traditional forty days had passed. He had then given his wife a sound beating and had threatened to throw her out of the house—though the one who should have been thrown out was Zarifa.

As it was impossible for Zarifa to go back to working in people's houses, she had no means of making a living other than the corncobs, unless her dream were fulfilled that her husband might return to her and the children, something for which she prayed daily.

On a very dark and inauspicious day something occurred that was not at all in her calculations. She awoke at dawn after a dreadful nightmare in which her husband had sprouted two green wings made of maize stalks and was carrying a large straw basket in which he collected up all the corncobs. He had then lifted off into the sky, putting out his tongue at her and laughing. She, meanwhile, was screaming at him and imploring him to return with the corncobs, but to no avail.

When she went out to her small plot to gather up the corncobs that had ripened, in preparation for roasting them as usual that afternoon, she found neither corncobs nor stalks. Instead she discovered that her plot had become a desolate wasteland, with municipality workers sprawled in a circle around pages of a national newspaper on which were stacked rounds of bread stuffed with beans and packets of pickles.

No sooner did Zarifa take in the scene, convinced that yesterday's nightmare had actually come to pass, than she beat her breast and shrieked, "Disaster!"

The workmen were astonished at the sight of this distraught woman in front of them. Some thought she was out of her mind, others imagined that some disaster was actually about to overtake them. The hungriest and laziest of them persuaded himself that the woman was merely seeking their aid in some matter, so he continued chewing away in peace.

"O Opener of the doors of sustenance, O All-knowing! What's up, woman?"

She pointed at her despoiled stalks of maize stacked nearby

on the ground, having been torn up by the roots, then at the hoes and mattocks lying beside them.

"Man, that's my daily bread and my children's. I'm ruined!"

Those who had thought she was off her head began to understand. One of them shouted at her angrily, "D'you think this is your family estate ,woman? By rights you should be in prison for trespassing on government property. By God, wonders never cease!"

Bitter tears flowed from Zarifa, and most of the men felt sorry for her and secretly cursed the government. They began to console her and to ask themselves: does she really make a living from selling the maize? Hasn't she got some other source of livelihood? When she told them her story, they advised her to look around for some other way of earning a living, at which she told them tearfully, "But the land's been here for five years and there's plenty of good Nile silt on it, and the government's not paid it the slightest attention, not for a single day."

The workers exchanged looks of perplexity: how can they explain to this woman standing before them about what goes on with the government? Should they say to her: another ten years might go by without the government cultivating the land, so long as there's no one in power or some person of importance to the government living in the district? Should they tell her that senior government employees dispose freely of authorized funds in special ways that suit their books? Should they inform her that the Agricultural Produce Company has paid bribes to those employees so that it can put up a huge store on the site of her piece of land in which to sell and market its canned goods?

Aware that she would never understand any of this, one of the men, thought a little and asked her where she lived. When she answered that she lived in the nearby shack with her children, he scratched his head and said, "Then go off and make us a pot of tea, may God reward you."

Readily agreeing, she returned after a while with the tea and poured it out into small glasses for them. While she was taking the money from them in payment, an idea occurred to her and she asked them whether they were going to carry on working in the area for some time.

"No, we've done our digging and that's it for us. Tomorrow, though, the construction men will begin work," one of them told her.

"The work's likely to go on for a year or more," added another.

She left them arguing among themselves and went back to her shack with the teapot and glasses, where she began giving serious thought to the idea of changing her business to serving tea to the workers who would be arriving the following day.

Several months after these incidents, winter having arrived with a vengeance, the American journalist returned to visit his girlfriend. He did not notice Zarifa as she distributed glasses of tea among the sewerage workers on the other side of the road. He was contemplating the secret of life's uninterrupted continuity over thousands of years in certain backward countries.

Snake Hunting

Mohamed Zefzaf

"I'm only an old woman, a widow," she said. "I've no children, no one in this world but God. If I don't defend myself, who will?"

"I'm frightened that one day one of the snakes will do for you," said a woman.

"If God means for a person to die, be it by the sting of a piece of rope, there's no one can stand against Him. And anyway, even though I kill so many snakes each year, the place still isn't rid of them."

She was well known for killing snakes. She had a special way of seeking them out under a pile of straw or a stone. She had bracelets made of snake skin, as well as belts, of various colors. The snakes' heads she would sell to itinerant druggists in exchange for sugar, tea, oil, or soap; she was told they were used in magic and sometimes for treating children, though she herself had never thought of employing magic, even for the sake of the person most close to her, her late husband. She knew that every sorceress came to a bad end: a broken leg, or blindness in both eyes, or the loss of a child or of livestock.

A woman carrying a basket filled with mud on her head looked at her. "Sister, I don't know how God gave you this courage and strength to attack snakes and vipers in their lairs."

"Why should I be afraid? As a child I saw my grandfather mount a horse in the middle of the night, as naked as God created Adam. Then he gave chase to a band of robbers who had come to steal our cows. He feared neither the cold nor the robbers' guns. At the end of that night I saw him firing down into the plain at the robbers. He returned home only when he'd got the cows back. My grandmother went and covered him up lest we see his nakedness. How can a woman like me with such a grandfather be afraid of snakes?"

The woman went off and left the old widow. Several parts of her body were wound round with variously colored snake skins. She was scattering seed to her chickens and calling to two cockerels that had strayed away from the rest. She dug her fingers into the ground and threw a clod of earth at the cockerels, which immediately joined up with the others. Their brilliant colors glistened under the sun's rays.

She would count her hens every two hours in case some snake or other animal—or even a human being—had passed by. More than forty years ago there had been foxes and wolves, but these had now completely disappeared. Perhaps they had been exterminated by the people who had built these scattered houses that were visited only at night in order to do things with the women there. The number of her hens had not grown less, nor would it do so, for she took care of them. She would sell one only when it had become plump. She was proud of the fact that her chickens were the plumpest and their eggs the biggest; the eggs of other people's hens were as small as pigeons' eggs or goat droppings.

143

She made her way toward the house built of mud and straw. Seeing Azzouz coming in her direction and getting down from his cart, she smiled to herself: she had thought of something to say to him that was likely to enrage him—though in fact he never got angry with her. Still several paces away from her, she heard him say, "And how are you, you old mouse? Still hunting snakes?"

"Men aren't capable of it. Do you remember when there were eight of you and just one snake was able to get the better of you and you were only able to kill it by drowning it? What sort of manliness was that? You became the laughingstock of your wives and daughters."

"Our mothers didn't suckle us on poison as yours did."

"What sort of manliness was that? The best of men, the best of all of you died and I wouldn't marry after he died. There's no man worth a nail paring of his."

"May God have mercy upon him! Why talk of those who have died, you old mouse?"

"Your wife's situation is no better than mine."

The two of them began to laugh. Then she threw down the dried-up branch she was carrying, brushed the dirt from her hands and wiped them on her gown.

"Have you been to Ain Diab?"

"Yes, but I left the cart on the track by the seashore and carried the two sacks of fodder on my back right up to the cart. I avoided the main road because you know what the police could do to me if they caught me."

"I do."

"We also needed a sack of sugar. We'll split it among us all—that's why I've come to you."

"Leave me a kilogram or two, though I don't have any money."

"Ever since the death of your husband you've been one of us.

144

When have we ever asked you for money? You can pay with a chicken. We can see about it later on when I've had a word with the gang."

Turning in the direction of the cart, he said, "If you need any fodder, we have some. You can come and take it or I'll send it to you with the girl Mannana."

At that moment she felt she wasn't really on her own. On the other hand, she would feel all alone when she thought about those accursed snakes that threatened her chickens the whole year round. When her chickens were attacked by some disease, that was God's decree and had nothing to do with anyone. But when she told herself that she was still capable of killing a snake, she felt assured that God would not one day let her die of hunger.

She had her own special way of hunting snakes. She would lie in wait for the snake whenever she heard her chickens cackling. Having discovered its hiding-place, she would quickly grab it by the tail and whirl it around and around in the air until it became dizzy, then bang it time and time again against a sharp piece of rock. When the rock was bespattered with blood and she felt the snake's body had lost all power of resistance, she would throw it to one side—but keep an eye on it from a distance. Seldom, though, did the snake's body make any movement, for she threw it aside only when she was certain it was dead. Sometimes a snake would make its escape and hide among the stones of the wall, though the old widow was quite capable of spending the whole day waiting for it to emerge.

She entered the house. Hearing someone outside calling "Auntie!" she immediately recognized the voice. She went out into the courtyard.

"Mannana!" called the old woman. "Come along, come nearer. Do you want an egg to boil?"

145

"My father sent you this nosebag," said the young girl. "It's full of fodder."

"Come along, come nearer."

The girl was barefoot, her head done up in a tattered kerchief. From her hand there dangled a nosebag made of doum-palm leaves, trailing along the ground. She rid herself of the nosebag and began scratching her backside, then her hair. The old woman noticed this and told her, "You're all dirty. You most likely don't let your mother wash you when she wants to. Your hair will get full of lice—and having a lot of lice shortens one's life. You've got to live a long time so you can marry and have some sons for your mother."

She approached the girl and took up the nosebag, hanging it on a wooden peg sticking out from the wall. Then she went into the house and came out with an egg in her hand, which she gave to the girl.

"Careful you don't break it."

"Do you still hunt snakes, Auntie?" Mannana said to her.

"They've disappeared these days. If I didn't do it, I wouldn't have a single live chicken."

"I'm frightened you'll be bitten one day by a snake."

"Don't be frightened—your auntie's still strong enough to kill all the snakes of Ouled Jerrar. Do you want me to boil the egg for you?"

"No, I'll boil it at home."

"Boil it and eat it on your own—and don't offer any of it to anyone."

"All right."

The young girl disappeared behind the trees that acted as a hedge around the old woman's house to the west. There was a mud oven over near the front door. Some hours ago she had put some dry charcoal in it and was now waiting for the pieces to catch fire. It was hard going, though, despite feeding it with kerosene. At first the flames had flared up, but this had had no effect on the dry charcoal. From time to time she would hear the crackling of flames coming from the mud oven and would go out and have a look at the pieces of charcoal in the hope they would have reddened, and several times she fanned the oven with a piece of tin and then blew on it. She put a pot on top of the oven, containing some sardines, carrots, and flour. She did not know who would be sharing the meal with her that day. Sitting on the hot sands, she heard the chickens cackling as they scattered, and she told herself that there must be a snake about. She got to her feet ready for action and went off in search of it. Her eyes bulged as she looked for it among the grasses. Behind her she heard Mannana's voice, "Auntie, is it a snake?"

She turned to her. "Haven't you gone home yet?"

"No, the egg broke."

"I told you so. Stay where you are so the snake doesn't bite you. I'll boil you another egg."

The chickens scattered in terror, jumping up onto the short reeds that grew around about. The old woman looked for some sign of the snake but could not find it. There was only a frog, its head tucked into its body, slowly hopping along.

"There's no snake," said the old woman, "—only a frog."

"Kill it like you kill the snakes," said the little girl.

"No, I don't kill frogs," said the old woman. "Come and kill it yourself. Come and learn how to kill frogs before killing snakes."

The little girl approached, looking at the fat frog.

"Pounce on it quickly," said the old woman, "and seize it by its legs and swing it around in the air till it's dizzy, then bang it against this sharp rock."

Mannana was timid, frightened, but some strong urge

spurred her on to pounce down and seize the frog by the leg. Then she began swinging it around and around like some rag toy, while the woman egged her on. "Go on, go on, it's not dizzy yet." Then Mannana banged the frog against the sharp piece of rock and its intestines spurted out, though its body still stirred in its death throes. The old woman went up close and looked down at the body, then pulled the child away by her hand.

"That's what I do with snakes. Now you'll wash your hands and I'll boil you an egg. Next time I'll teach you how to kill a snake."

The Money Order

Mohamed El-Bisatie

They are both very aged. They sit on the wooden balcony from early morning when the small square in front of them is still empty, and the basin of the dilapidated fountain at its center is filled with dried leaves that have been blown there by the night's squalls.

With the passage of the years, the wooden balcony has tilted considerably and has had supports placed under it to prevent it from collapsing.

The old couple sit on chairs facing each other: the man, plump and flabby, is dressed in a short-sleeved, white *gallabiya* and wields a fly-whisk; the woman's meager frame is draped in a blue or red satin dress with large flowers.

They let down a basket to passing vendors as they have their breakfast on the balcony. When the sun climbs, they go inside and close themselves in. By late afternoon they are back on the balcony.

At the beginning of every month they receive a money order that is brought to them at noon by the employee from the post office. During all the seven years in which their son has been away, the man has never been late: they wait for him on the balcony and he places the money order in the basket, along with the book for a signature to say they have received it. After her husband has signed it, the woman scrutinizes the book, for he often signs in the wrong place.

They go out immediately after receiving the money order, having prepared their going-out clothes the night before. These she has placed on two chairs in the living room, and has cleaned his shoes, with his socks rolled up inside them. It is the only day in the month when they go out. The man puts off collecting his pension until the money order arrives, then he cashes them both together.

He puts on a loose-fitting linen coat that gives out a smell of mothballs, and tucks a handkerchief around the collar of his shirt as he has done ever since he was headmaster at the elementary school. He stands waiting impatiently for her by the open door until she has finished her makeup. She puts a lot of kohl on her eyes, pulls from her cheeks some wisps of hair she did not notice the previous night, and applies dark red lipstick before joining him, and he descends the stairs leaning on her. When they come out into the street, he removes his arm and they walk along side by side.

Having finished at the post office, he gives her the money and says, "Don't forget the toothpicks and the camphor oil."

"You don't have to remind me every time."

"And the cigarettes?"

"And the cigarettes."

She buys him a packet of cigarettes, for once in a while when suffering from insomnia he smokes a cigarette. They walk for a while in a neglected garden with no seats and with leafless trees that give little shade, and when they are wet with perspiration they go off to the station. Overcome by fatigue, she settles him down in a seat far from the crowds, with a napkin on his chest, and then goes to bring the ice cream.

The shop is behind them. She crosses the passageway in a few steps and comes back holding a couple of tubs. When they have devoured them quickly, the woman says, "This time he's got cones. You like them."

"Yes."

The woman goes to the shop and returns with two cones filled with ice cream.

"Better than the tubs," the man says.

The trains come to a stop then go on. People get off and on. A lot of noise and children running about. The two of them are silent, looking around them. When things quieten down and the station is almost empty, the woman rises to her feet and says, "Cone or tub?"

"Cone."

So deep is the silence that descends on the station that they hear the coughing of the employees in their offices on the second floor.

"How many trains have passed?" says the man, fighting against sleep.

"Six."

"Five."

"You didn't count the goods train."

"No, I didn't. Do you think the pension's going to be enough?"

"The same question once again!"

"What d'you mean, once again?"

"You ask it every time, and I know what you're going to say next."

"And what am I going to say?"

"You're going to ask me what would happen if the money order stopped coming."

"That's right. What if it did?"

"And what would stop it?"

"Just suppose that it did."

"I don't want to suppose."

"It's many long years since he came."

"He has his reasons."

"There aren't even any letters. He used to send a letter with the money order. He doesn't any more."

"He's rushed. Perhaps he doesn't have pen and paper at the time."

"And who doesn't carry a pen and paper in his pocket?"

"You don't."

She says that she is going to bring more ice cream, that this is the last time, and after that they'll go back home. He says that he will wait for the four o'clock train, that it is the best one of all.

They fall into a doze and wake to the gentle sound of the rails shaking. He sees it coming, the four o'clock train, speeding along noiselessly, with its shining, polished carriages and its closed glass windows with faces staring out from behind them. Few people get off or on. It stops for a while, then continues on its way.

The woman helps him to his feet and the two of them leave the station.

To the Night's Shelter

Mohamed Khudayir

W ith the approach of winter I have to look around for
a secure lair, a night-time shelter that will not eject
me too early of an evening. This is an indoor café, so
small it houses no more than a few dirtied chairs amid the
ancient woodwork. This café remains generally the last refuge
of a night after the other indoor souk cafés have closed their
doors one by one. It may now be eight or nine o'clock, or it
may be late, for only two young men are sitting in the café not
far from my table; they are sitting in the front part of the café,
the part wholly open to the edge of the passageway of the souk
that has begun to bolt its doors and is stealing away and disappearing, emptying itself unobserved. I may sit for a long time
in this café, but the outdoor cafés don't interest me. Here I sit
in the place I want, exactly facing the windows of an upper
story of a hotel across the souk's passageway; to be precise,
opposite an open window, the sole one among the numerous
sets of closed windows that gives out any light. I follow the
hotel lodgers as they return singly and ascend the stairs that

start right at its entrance onto the souk, to the top floor where all the bedrooms are situated.

The two young men beside me are blind; they cover that spent area of their faces, the empty cavities, with black spectacles, and each of them has placed his stick against the edge of the table. One of them has a lute wrapped in a cloth bag, which he has rested between his feet against the legs of the table. They do not sit opposite one another across the table but in opposing directions, on the two sides of the table, in postures whereby one of them has his back to the souk passageway and is leaning on the table, while the other raises his head with a slight backward movement in the direction of the solitary illuminated hotel window, which is to say, being precise, in the direction in which I am watching him. He makes no movement as a piercing beam of light, a sharp reflection, penetrates his darkened spectacles.

I have become used to seeing them at this time every evening, usually sitting in this self-same position. Doubtless they have discovered, with their darkened inner senses, that like them I frequent this café and that at this very moment I am sitting close to them. Yet I know better than they do the whereabouts of the owner at the back of the café, sitting alongside the stove. Also, more than they, I fall under the sway of the mirror that occupies the whole length of the rear wall of the café, making a picture of the backs of our heads lost among the empty chairs, tables, and posters, the commemorative flags, and the outlines of the souk. I and the shining mirror, redolent with the steam of the last brewing of tea, exchange surveillance through the lighted window of the hotel that opens onto it like a quicksilver eye trained on my back.

The two blind men are talking; one of them, the man leaning on the table, is talking uninterruptedly. "And so it is that, at specific times, at those moments when I'm in a low state, I stay on in bed for a whole day, even two days, without performing any action except to turn my body from side to side, from the edge of the bed to the wall and from the wall to the edge of the bed. I raise myself slightly, then let my body fall. Then I go back to tossing and turning and do nothing but pull out my clothes that have accumulated under me and hamper my movement in the bed. Yesterday I slept through the whole of the day, and if you hadn't woken me I'd have slept through all today as well. Do you know that? In actual fact I sensed you approaching me and leaning over, and I prepared myself for your hand, which started feeling its way to my shoulder. It was just as well you did this, as otherwise I'd have slept through all of today as well."

The other blind man is motionless, facing the open lighted window amid the rows of windows whose wooden filigree shutters have been lowered, all of which form the hotel frontage that overlooks the souk and the café. The light also infiltrates through the holes in the sloping shutters of three windows adjoining the open one. These four windows belonging to a single front room lie to the right of the hotel entrance. There is a similar number of unlit windows on the other side. The open window divulges the contents of the room: a clothes horse, the top of a mirror, a wooden ceiling, then half the figure of a man wearing an undershirt and with a loincloth round his middle. The man places on the windowledge a cigarette he has between his fingers and begins to take off his undershirt. His raised arms disappear behind the windowframe in his attempt to extricate them from the undershirt. The skin of his chest is tautened over his prominent ribs, and his stomach, pressed downward, is contracted. From here I see the ridges of his smooth, pale chest, the hair of his armpits, his nipples, the brown spots and burns, the sunken navel: an insectile mass, crucified within the frame of the window. The man bends forward in a final attempt to be rid of the garment, then he hurls it to some place in the room, spreads his loincloth on the windowsill, after taking up his cigarette from it, and moves away inside the room. After that he appears for only brief moments inside the frame, crossing the room or seating himself. His unknown movements throw up incomplete constituents of himself, from the top of his shoulders, his chest, and back, as he bends, turns around, sits down, or stands up. When the fleeting, amputated pieces of the man in the room disappear from view, my attention is drawn to the clothes horse weighted down with shirts, trousers, and towels. Suddenly the light in the room goes out and the windows darken. Perhaps the man has taken himself off to bed.

The blind man who is leaning on the table continues. "Normally I feel a great emptiness in my head. This emptiness becomes greater after a long sleep: a soothing emptiness that gently and continually pushes against the walls of my head. Every movement has an intensely clear echo to it. For those who have lost their sight such an echo becomes a loud, whistling reverberation. Thus it was that I was able to become sharply observant and to pick up the softest of sounds from around about me and to determine where they come from. I am likewise capable of imagining the movements taking place in the darkness as they advance toward me, creeping along like a swarm of reptiles. Yes, the tiniest things mingle in my head and come together in a single, uninterrupted reverberation, just as the melodies and the violin merge into a single rhythm, and the dancer's arms and her castanets come together in a single dance. Darkness and silence in a single room, in one continuous whistling. And you and I, too, in a single room. Thousands of dusty feet, of pulsating vibrations, I hear them advancing toward my bed. In a daze I meet them, preparing my trembling body for them, like the hollow of a tree, like a vast sandy pit.

Uneasy moments pass, after which I have a sensation of being filled with the things that are light, silent, and unknown. I go back to sleep. Is it sleep? I don't know exactly if that slow falling backward is sleep. Neck pains. The heavy ceiling. Being crammed into a narrow box strewn with garbage."

Meanwhile, the blind man who raises his face toward the window where the light has been turned off follows the last lodger, who has climbed the hotel stairs to his room. (The lodger slows down midway up the stairs, the stairs that are generally dark, then continues his ascent, running his hand over the wall, while he counts to himself the stairs that remain for him to reach the top story. After halfway the stairs curve around and place the lodger all of a sudden at the beginning of a long corridor, on both sides of which lie the guests' rooms. The first room on the right. He opens the door and advances into the room's darkness toward his bed, then sits on the edge of it and begins to take off his clothes while yawningly examining the faces of those with whom he is sharing the room.)

The blind man who is leaning on the table proceeds. "Sometimes I wake up suddenly. I wake up as though I'd never been to sleep. I sit on my bed, that is to say I dangle my feet from the bed and sit on the edge, and I listen for the impact of that thing that has woken me. I mean of course the stick, believing as I do that the stick walks about the room on its own. I am convinced that someone or something walks about the room. He and the stick. I stretch out my hand to where I generally put my stick beside the bed. I stretch out my hand but don't find it in its place. The stick naturally moves with unhurried steps. Of course the tread has ceased. When I wake up the stick will have come to a stop. I hear the stick because I have not wholly rid myself of the shackles of sleep. I stretch out my hand so as to get to my feet, but I don't find my stick. I bend down to search for my sandals because I want to go to the lavatory. I stretch out my hand and bend down and my head bumps against something. I believe it's a table. I have said that there's little furniture in the room, that there's no furniture, that it's empty. Then I get to my feet without a stick and search for the door, and though I discover the door I don't go out. I return to my place, seat myself on the bed and listen. I am unable to walk without a stick. This is the curse that has been placed upon us. The stairs and the opening to the lavatory, and the crumbling floor that will collapse, the damp parts that must be avoided and not stepped on. Were you in the room? I thought it was you who were walking about, finding your way with your stick. Did you hear me when I said, 'Who's that?' And yet no one answered. Then the pacing stopped completely. Did you return to your bed? Yes, I forgot your bed on the other side of the room. So, in addition to my bed, there's your bed and the table. Are there other things in our room? No, as far as I know there's nothing else. How many paces do you reckon there are between our two beds? Have you tried to make the calculation? One day I tried to: twenty-five paces. Can you imagine how spacious our room is! A room spacious only in length. Sometimes I have the sensation I'll take a hundred paces before reaching the other end of it, and yet I don't do so. An empty room. That's how I imagine it. Next to the hotel facade that faces the café are adjoining wooden facades with windows covered by separate awnings, bordered by facades with windows with contiguous awnings. Then you don't see the subsequent facades because they are as follows: rectangles of windows without shutters, then rectangles of windows with separate shutters that curve around with the souk passageway and are cut through by alleys. Yet I imagine the similar hidden facades with connected awnings, and so on. Also, fenced rooftops, and open rooftops, and narrow winding alleys, and wooden darkness, then watery darkness, yellow darkness, and so on."

Talking in a lower voice, the blind man continues, "Sometimes I feel it's a very narrow room. I tried to play a tune slowly: one stroke of the string, a stroke strong and repeated. It comes out loud and bulky, like heavy footsteps on a cellar paving. Did you hear how strong the stroke on the string was when it's repeated over and over? For a long time I went on striking the one string, a string that plunges into the flesh with incisive intonation. The stroke rebounds from the walls, as though I'm in a room narrower than a small box. Every string is a blind man or a blind woman: hollowed out, taut, expectant. When we strike all the strings, the heap of blind people stirs and leaves the belly of the lute in a rumbling clamor. Then it leaves the room for the streets and is swallowed up by the night. But striking only one string invites but a single blind girl, supple and pliant, to dance; she moves in practiced rotations among the group of blind people lurking in the belly of the instrument, silent as idols. The blind dancer may leave the belly, but she does not go far away from it, for she is tightly bound to the one who controls her fate by a strong, delicate string by means of which, at the termination of the dance, he draws her back to her place among the blind. This is my concept about striking a single string. Is there anyone still in the café? I don't believe there's anyone but us in it. I hear no voice. This meat, I don't think it was sufficiently cooked. What's the time now? Someone must tell us what the time is."

The blind man who is facing the window is still following the footsteps of the last lodger. (This lodger has acquired the habit of counting the stairs as he ascends—twenty steps. He has likewise acquired the habit, particularly during the last few nights, of slowing down halfway up the stairs, then coming to a halt at the tenth stair, where fingers of light coming from the top of the staircase join up with those infiltrating through from the bottom of the staircase, and he leans against the wall. In this area of shadow, as has been his habit during the last few nights, he undoes his shirt buttons and feels with his fingertip a dark-colored pointed place high up his chest: a firm body that throbs. After that he continues on his winding ascent. When he enters his room, the first one to the right, he approaches the bed in the darkness and stands for some moments in hesitation about exposing his small throbbing secret on his chest. He examines the faces of the slumbering lodgers and begins cautiously to take off his clothes.)

The blind man who is leaning on his table says, "I don't believe the meat was cooked enough."

After a moment's pause, which causes me to turn toward them, he continues to speak. "Anyone seeing us like this, inseparable night and day, would take us for brothers. We walk together or one of us supports the other. We carry my lute. They would regard us as lucky because we work in a place of entertainment: nights of gaiety, noisy with music. Night never ends for those working in places of entertainment. Perhaps each of us has a close relationship with one of the dancers. Dinners and kind words, not from pity but by reason of blind art, the power of the black phantom of music. So very many songs and lethal delights and limitless profanations. And so very few subterfuges and meannesses. Nothing wrong with that. Sometimes there's the giddiness that fells one to the ground, and the drum that dins into one's head: the utter tiredness. No matter. And sometimes the filth and squalor."

The blind man concludes all this with a short dry laugh, while the silent blind man follows his last lodger across the darkness of the unlit window opposite. (That thing grows, it sits on the lodger's chest like some hirsute animal, speechless, and begins to lick his face with its tongue, then it gives an imperceptible leap, leaving a dark aperture in its place. The lodger sits up straight in the bed and examines the room: it's an irregular room, possessing a fifth corner, toward which the beds, the walls, and the ceiling tilt. This tilt makes him rise to his feet with great caution lest his bed should shift and swoop down toward the extra corner, and he takes up from a table in the middle of the room a plastic water jug and places its mouth to his own. From the window he sees sections of parapets and rooftops and a deep slice of sky. The lodger goes out to the corridor and the door closes with a bang he is unable to stifle. He stops behind the door and listens: the footsteps, lingering in the silence, and the slamming of the door, will unsettle the stability of the beds; they will be swept away and will be piled up one on top of the other in the sloping corner. But this collapse will not upset the lodgers in the room, for their flaccid cheeks and greasy faces are at rest on the softness of pillows, and their hands are squeezed between their thighs, or lie slack on their chests, stifling slight pulsations. These are the brethren of the room, absent as of now; they do not anticipate the breaking in of hunting dogs appearing from the roofs and taking up lodging in their beds, nor does it occur to them that robbers are this very minute on their way from the suburbs, nor are they frightened by the slaps and ravings of senile women beggars who will drag them from their beds and hurl them outside. The lodger moves, then follows his shadow toward the end of the corridor. The doors on both sides are ajar. The rooms to the right are numbered 1 to 6, starting from the lodger's room, and are faced on the other side by rooms numbered 7 to 12; the sole room that is without a number lies at the end of the corridor and has perhaps been made into a storeroom. At its end the corridor branches out into two forks that lead to the toilets. There are mirrors above the washbasins in a small open space that also contains low wall-urinals, in some of which dark yellow urine has been obstructed where cigarette ends have been thrown. The lodger washes his hands and face, then dries them with the tail of his pajama jacket. When he pulls the two ends of the jacket in front of one of the mirrors, the red fruit hanging from his ribs comes into view, floating on the pale yellow skin, throbbing, growing, soft and ripe, with a tapered head. He scrutinizes it carefully. After a while this 'thing' will dash off like some small animal, unnoticed, leaving a dark aperture in its place, and will begin its customary nightly stroll through the streets, the courtyards, the bridges, and garbage bins, then it will return at dawn, will knock at the lodger's ribs, and attach itself to them. The lodger has returned to his room. The other lodgers are visible through the half-open doors, asleep in a soft glow, their feet pushing the light coverings to the ends of the beds. They stir, they toss and turn and groan in a fierce struggle against their hirsute animals crouching on their chests, while their shoes and slippers, which they have left under the beds, run about in their rooms making a noise. And in their struggle their clothes are pulled aside from their thighs and hairy genitals. Their mouths are open, though they may close tight from time to time, when their teeth grind in rage like saws. One of them wakes up breathless, almost choking from a dry cough that resembles a dog's barking. The lodger comes to a stop in front of the door of his room at the beginning of the corridor; he listens, then gently pushes the door and enters. He sits on the edge of his bed and examines his silent companions in their sleep. He stretches out and pulls the cover over himself. Before he nods off, the sound of running feet seeps into his head.)

I was about to leave the café, and turned around in search of the owner. However, I stayed on. The blind man was continuing his discourse, cloaked in deeper darkness. "Someone must tell us the time. Shall we go? Time is on our side. All is night. All is darkness. All is wakefulness. All is silence. All is descending. All is a twisting and turning. All is heaviness. All is wakefulness. All is sleep. Shall we go? Our room is not far from the café. The third alleyway to the left, after the second alleyway to the right, and before that of course the first alleyway forking off from the short alleyway that forks off from the souk. We know our way: the alleyways and their walls guide our steps. Over there is a dip rather like a puddle of water or the opening of a sewer sump. We're not sure. A few steps away is a large barrel that is always empty. Usually one of our sticks strikes against it. It resounds. This no longer frightens or disconcerts us. Doubtless they are behind doors listening to the thump of the stick. Behind the first door I hear the sound of an old man coughing or complaining of some pain or other. I also hear the sewing machine behind the second door. As for the third door, it muffles the barking of a puppy that appears to be locked in a room or chained up under the stairs. That old man behind the first door I believe to be deaf, or perhaps he's totally paralyzed in his chair, the seat of which has sunk under him, as he directs a fixed stare at a crack in the wall in front of him, or at a picture, at the shadow of some specter that takes on visible form before him: the specter of himself in the time of his youth when he was a runner, a horseman, or a soldier, then when he became a butcher or a pawnbroker. As for that puppy, it whines more than it barks, as though it has a thorn stuck in the tender pad of its paw. No doubt it has been squeezed into some narrow den, its neck encircled by a chain that chokes it further still when it rushes forward toward the scent of the children of the family, all of whom have taken to their beds. From the fourth or fifth door there emanate sounds

163

of an endless quarrel and the shouting of children. There, behind one of these two doors, is a large family numbering some twenty or thirty persons. There is a man there who works as a hawker selling boiled turnips or beans on a barrow that he goes around with to workshops and cinemas. The woman is his wife and works as a cleaner at a school or as a street sweeper. Perhaps there is a second or third wife. They always hit upon something to quarrel about at the end of the day. A group of the boys work as bootblacks, cigarette sellers, or apprentices in a small blacksmith's workshop, and they generally talk about money. The remaining children are young and should be accorded greater attention, for they are extremely filthy. It is not only a matter of cleanliness; there is also their low standard at lessons, their emaciated state, and other things. Conversations are interrupted and lost amid ceaseless screaming. These sounds grow fainter the further we penetrate inside. If there is a sixth, a seventh, an eighth, a ninth or a tenth door, life is completely extinguished behind them, and I no longer hear anything but the impact of our two sticks. Or they are behind them hearing us as we approach and they keep silent until we have passed by. Here are the inseparable specters, the children say inwardly: they'll bump into something and collapse over each other in a heap in the alleyway. As for the women, they yawn and get up to go to bed, then dream of blind men smitten by the cold going around and around from alleyway to alleyway after losing their way to the shelter. But the walls curve off and lead our steps to our shelter, which lies in the depths of the final cul-de-sac. This door needs no more than a slight push for it to open. So—shall we go?"

I have crossed the souk passageway as I make my way to the hotel entrance facing the café. I am accustomed to counting the steps. In the middle of the stairway, at the tenth step, I come to a stop in the area of shade. I rest my back for an instant against the wall, then continue my ascent, with the stairway curving around and placing me suddenly at the opening of the corridor of rooms. My bedroom is the first on the right. My tired steps lead me to it. I push the door and advance into the darkness of the room toward my bed, then I seat myself on the edge of it and start taking off my clothes while, yawning, I examine the faces of the lodgers who are sharing the room with me.

The Man Shouldn't Know of This

Hanan al-Shaykh

I didn't need to look at my watch: when my heartbeats quicken I know that the time has come and that I must get ready, so I enter the bathroom and whisper a word or a sentence to the mirror.

All the time the warm water comes down on me, I give myself up to it with a delightful sense of relaxation. I only turn off the flow from the tap when I remember the pot of pink cream with its scent that penetrates right to the pores of my skin. Then I hasten to dry my body. A few small hairs on my thighs, like herbage in a marsh, detain me. I think about plucking them out with tweezers, but I change my mind for they are scarcely visible. I put cream on my body and rub it in leisurely, reaching all over, feeling that my limbs are alive and giving off their own sensations. This state they are in, while taking different forms, shifts between love and the expression of it in an atmosphere of intimacy. I turn around, trying to gather up that self of mine that flies around in parts of the room, that self that strays between experiences of the past and the hallmark they have left

166

on me, and my fear of them, and between thinking of relin-
quishing this habit of mine of preparing myself and the fear I
have of this love. It is as though I am a blind man going down
stairs without a stick. Yet I must curb my desire, for the very
moment I see him before me—as he meets me and I hear his
voice and we sit down and talk and I see his words issuing out
of his throat and through his teeth and I know that his neck is
warm—I tremble and ask for nothing more than that he embrace
and enter me. However, I sit pretending to disregard what is
happening to me and attempt to concentrate the whole of me on
what he is saying—but the words enter my ear and go from it to
my brain, which orders them to descend to my lips, to my neck,
to my breast, to my stomach, to my back, to the base of my
spine, and I become paralyzed.

And so it is every time I meet him: I am lost in expectation,
between hurrying and proceeding slowly. I sit and all of me is a
desire to plunge headlong behind this feeling that has control of
me, hesitating between moving back and continuing on. I sit,
and it is as if I am a sparrow trembling on barbed wire, fearing
to move as it prepares itself for flight, the wire pricking it. I try
not to fight against my desire for him, and I go on, and the
whole of me is a belief that our physical contact is a comple-
ment to talking, is talking itself. Yet I retreat as I appraise from
the way he is sitting, from the way he takes my hands between
his, from the heat of the palm of his hand, from the belt of his
trousers, from his socks even, from the way he brings his glass
close up to his lips—as I appraise from all this that he is happily content to exchange stories, feelings, and news.

When we have fitted closely into one another, it is as if we
are a single sheet of paper that has been folded just the once. As
I touch his neck with my lips, the pulse of his neck lingers
between my lips, then travels down my throat to my belly, to my

whole being. I begin to shiver as I wish that he might possess the whole of me in a single moment, and it is as if I am a piece of charcoal that wishes to attract a spark as it fears the drops of water advancing upon it. So he looks at me in surprise at what is happening, seeing my teeth—whose symmetry he has long admired—being drawn tight together, as I prefer to grind them rather than let the words expressing my desire for him—and my urgency—slip from them.

I put on a record as the final stage of my preparations; I wait while the effect of the music begins. Then I sink back inertly on the bed, bring my arm up to my nose and smell it; in moments he is close by me; I whisper a word to him and conclude our conversation by fondling myself, stopping only when I let out a slight, shuddering cry. I grant my body moments of calm before looking at my watch. I get up, aware that there is only half an hour left before I am to meet him. Should I take the underground or a taxi?

The Day Grandpa Came

Mahmoud Al-Wardani

At the cool, shady entrance to the house, Mustafa stood leaning his shoulder against the rough wall next to his balcony on the first floor and watched them as they played football in the small lane. The lane was cut off on the south by a low house whose windows were closed against the blazing heat of a cruel sun, in whose rays the boys seemed to float as they leapt about. Mustafa was wishing that these older boys would finish their game so that those of his own age could rush down right away and occupy the ground. In front of each house were a number of boys watching the game from the cool darkness of the entrances to their homes.

To the left of him the lane was open to Kitchener Street, the wide street that led to the one with all the crazy trucks traveling northward, while the trains, the other side of the fence, never stopped their whistling and clattering.

He spotted the horse-drawn carriage as it approached, swaying slightly, from the direction of the hospital and stopped right in front of the lane. The ash-gray horse was restless under the

169

burning sun and shook its neck up and down continuously in short movements.

With his back to Mustafa, the old man got down from the carriage and began to collect himself together before turning around to face him, with his white beard the color of milk and his red tarbush that shimmered inside the folds of the snow-white shawl wound round it. He moved slowly, his dark-colored stick dangling from his wrist. Adjusting the position of the three bags he was holding, he stomped along in his loose-fitting overcoat.

He looked all around him, appearing apprehensive as he almost collided with the players in the lane, which he had to cross in order to reach the other side. He tried to keep hold of the bags in his arms, while the stick jerked up and down just above the ground.

Mustafa had straightened up and moved a few steps away from the entrance, then stopped. —It's my grandpa, Sheikh Hashem, Mustafa said to himself, as he made an effort to bring him vaguely to mind. —It's him, it's grandpa! A long time ago we left grandpa's house in Mansoura and came back to Cairo. Then we lived in many different houses before settling down here close to the railway. Do you remember me, grandpa? I remember when I would laugh at you when I saw your rosy face smiling at me. My mother will be happy. I can see her bursting into tears when she meets you.

Reaching the end of the lane, the old man turned in the direction of the children gathered behind the two stones set apart to indicate the goal. He bent down to one of the boys in the blazing sun, moving his head and his mouth. The boy made a sign toward the house, so he rearranged the three bags in his arms and went on his way. Passing close by Mustafa, he went into the dark stairway. He coughed as his stick gave the ground several short taps.

—So, how did you know we lived here, grandpa? Yes, you're my grandpa, even though you passed right by me as you entered, and I was looking at you and you didn't recognize me. I saw your rosy face and that white beard of yours that I love encircling your face, and your loose clothes that are slightly damp at the neck. I remember all right. Two years have passed while I've been at school since you last came from Mansoura. You came once when I was in the third year and now I'm in the fifth.

Mustafa took the stairs at a run. At the door of the darkened flat he veered off to the hall, from the half-opened doors of which people were calling out to one another. He looked into the door of his family's room and saw his mother crying and muttering in a choked voice, with her face all twitching. His grandfather was laughing and saying in his hoarse, raucous voice, "How are you, my girl Kareema? How are you, girl?"

Before making a place for himself on the sofa, which was covered with a faded blue sheet and rested against the wall close to the open door, he removed his turban and chose a clean place for it alongside him. Then he spotted Mustafa and his face beamed with joy, and he opened his arms as he guffawed. "Come here, Sheikh Mustafa—in the name of God, who would believe it!"

Shy to begin with, the boy stepped toward him before rushing forward into his embrace. He breathed in the clean, dark-colored overcoat his grandfather was wearing. His head turned as he gave himself up to the arms encircling his shoulders. The old man patted his head and kissed him on the forehead.

"Where's Muna, Sheikh Mustafa? By God, you've grown!" he exclaimed.

The boy was trapped in the narrow space between the bed and the sofa. He could hear the voices of the boys at play through the open balcony. The room seemed to him cramped, with his mother sitting on the floor beside the door, after taking the serving tray out from under the bed. She was wearing a light *gallabiya* of pale mauve with short sleeves and had a white kerchief tied around her head. There was only a very tiny space between the bed and the cupboard that stood next to the door, where she had lit the spirit stove and placed the kettle on it. Crying and trembling, she had propped herself against the cupboard and heard it give a sudden cracking noise. She allowed her gaze to rest on the two of them as she smiled.

"How are you, grandpa?" said Mustafa. "I've missed you—and my aunts, and my uncle, too."

"By God, you've grown, Sheikh Mustafa," said his grandfather with a laugh. "And the girl Muna, has she grown as much as you?"

"I'll bring her to you right away, grandpa," Mustafa answered.

He slipped away from him and was almost running when his grandfather called out, "Wait, man, . . . wait."

Putting his hand into a bag beside him, he brought out a fine yellow banana, whose aroma filled the room. Mustafa turned back again, seizing hold of the banana, but his grandfather continued to call out, "Steady, Sheikh Mustafa . . . . Steady . . . . Take it easy."

Undoing the buttons of the overcoat, he plunged his hand inside and took out a dark, creased leather wallet. He opened it up and produced a new ten-piaster note and pressed it into Mustafa's hand.

Mustafa turned around again, clutching the banana and the ten-piaster note.

Entering the hallway, he was surrounded by darkness. He made his way to the room of Umm Fatima, the mute woman; he found the door ajar and the room empty.

—But how did you get here, grandpa? After my father died, my grandfather and my uncle came with the big van that looked like an elephant, and the porters filled it up with the many things that were in the house: the contents of a living room, a dining room, and a bedroom. They took us to Mansoura. We lived with them and they piled up our things in the small flat downstairs.

He retraced his steps and walked to Sayyid's room, Umm Nagat's son. Umm Nagat, who was squatting on the mattress plucking the *mulukhiya* leaves off their stalks, said, "There are devils up above at Umm Mohamed's."

She drew her legs together, pulled down her *gallabiya*, which had ridden up slightly, and smiled. "Who have you got with you, Mustafa?"

Leaning his shoulder against the door, he answered, "My grandfather . . . . I was looking for Muna."

Before waiting for her answer he stepped back and went out. He jumped down the stairs, then came to a stop at the front door with the boys who were watching the game. Mustafa remembered how the first year after his father's death had passed. —My mother didn't know a moment's peace: my grandfather's dark-skinned wife used to scream at us—at me and Muna, my sister—whenever she saw us.

His heart was beating; he was breathless and could scarcely make out the players in front of him, nor yet the other boys who were around him. He did, however, see a boy close by gesturing to him.

"Mustafa," yelled the boy, "There was an old man who was asking about your mother."

"Yes, it's my grandfather," said Mustafa with a nod of his head.

He found himself darting through the lane, then crossing

Kitchener Street to the main street with the crazy traffic going northward while the trains were whistling and making a din and creaking as they slowed down at the gates close to Cairo's main station.

—We used to eat with my mother in our room alone. I wasn't able to talk to my grandfather and laugh with him as I wanted. In fact, when my aunts had come back from school, my grandfather's wife would make me keep to our tiny, overcrowded flat, which I didn't like, until they had finished doing their homework. As for Muna, she was frightened of my grandfather's wife and would stay the whole time with my mother.

Mustafa reminded himself that he had to look for his sister Muna. The flaming sun, mixed with the sticky smell of exhaust fumes and heavy dust, stung him.

He turned back and started running again.

He told himself, "It was in the year when we had returned to Cairo that you dropped in on us, Grandpa—I don't know how. How did you know where our house was? We lived in so many, many houses before we settled in this room in Abdurrahman Khalil Alley."

He found himself going up the stairs and approaching the door of the flat. In the hallway he could hear the raucous voice of his grandfather gently saying to his mother, "Listen to what I'm saying—I know what's best for you."

His mother's voice was choked, so he brought his head closer in order to make out exactly what was going on. He was frightened.

"And the children?" he heard his mother replying.

"The man agrees to take both you and the children," he said slowly.

The mother ended the conversation by suddenly standing up,

174

as she shouted, "Right from the beginning if I'd wanted . . . . A man who's a stranger to my children—no, not a man who's a stranger to my children."

He heard his grandfather mumbling and shaking his head, but his mother interrupted him by answering, "I didn't ask a thing of you, nor from anyone else . . . ."

He saw his grandfather immersed in the confined light of the balcony, squatting on the sofa in his cotton caftan with its pale stripes, with his overcoat beside him, clean and buttoned up, and his bright red turban on top of it with the white shawl wound around it, lying near the three paper bags. His grandfather was not looking at his mother as he spoke to her. She sat with her back against the bed at a distance from him.

Mustafa's eyes met his mother's and he saw that they were bathed in tears and that her face was flushed. He turned to her, without looking at his grandfather, and said, "Muna's upstairs at Umm Mohamed's . . . . I'm going up to see her."

Then he went out.

My Fellow Passenger

Ibrahim Samouiel

B oth the gesticulations he made and the reptilian hissing sound that came out of his mouth made me think that the person beside me in the bus was out of his mind. His face, when I snatched a hasty glance at it, was expressionless, as though concealing within it a land mine set to explode in accordance with the number of my seat. I tried to distance myself by looking out of the window at the road whizzing by on the other side of the bus.

"Man, it's enough to make you go crazy!"

I was taken unawares by the quavering voice, not realizing that it was addressing me. It was the voice of the man sitting by me, next to the window. I affected a smile as I looked at him but he merely continued to direct his words at me with intoxicated eyes.

"I swear to you, by God, my mind simply flipped. For ten years we were like lovebirds. Not for a day did I spare any pains or say 'No'—the Devil take it!"

He accentuated what he was saying by slapping his thigh. He

then drew his hand along the extent of his leg and back as he leaned forward then sat bolt upright.

In order to check the flow of words I said, "It turned out all right, God willing? It seems . . ."

He turned his face toward the window so that his voice was reflected back to me, muffled by the glass. "Yes, we've come to accept that life's become costly. As you yourself say, my dear woman, one just can't believe the cost of things. Fine, what I mean, Fadwa, is that . . ." He turned toward me and the troubled look on his face scared me. "What I mean, man, is if life's all that expensive—the Devil take it! It's a disaster! By God, don't you think it's a disaster?"

I nodded my head, having it in mind to jump in and say something, but he rushed on. "As if we didn't have enough to cope with! Isn't it enough that we're leading this lousy life? The first birth, then the second, and the third time she had twins—four children needing a sackful of money spent on them. What with their mother and me, it makes six of us. Then there's the rent for the house. You wouldn't be far wrong if you called it a chicken coop. No, sir. Reckon it at twelve hundred liras from the company and eight hundred for working after office hours at Abu Majid's shop. What shall I do? Cut myself into little pieces?"

Seizing the chance to answer him, I said, "Sir, that's how things are, but . . ."

He didn't make room for me to continue, most likely didn't even hear me.

"So the house is leaking—shall we put patches on it? The kids are naked and no better off than their father. We're in need of a thousand and one things. That's a fact. But, as the proverb has it, we go on trimming away at the squab's feathers till we get ourselves a fully-fledged pigeon. Yes, we go on making do with what we've got, but what else can we do? What, indeed!

Hassan—now he's with me at the company, a hard worker just like me. He really is. But Hassan smuggles things in addition to the job he does after his regular work. Man, God be my witness, I wouldn't know how to smuggle a day-old chick! No, sir—nor how to flog watches and jeans. Brother, they cleaned me out. I tried, and they took me to the cleaners. I don't deny it. That's what happened. What's the point of lying? We've landed up completely broke. But what did she think she was going to do . . . ?"

His voice broke and he buried his face against the glass as though attempting to penetrate it. I was at a loss to understand what he was saying. I found myself intrigued by his irrational chatter. I tried to guess what it was all about and became even more lost. I leaned my head against the back of the seat, then took out my cigarettes and offered him one. "It can't be all that bad, man. Have a smoke and blow it away."

"By God," he stated, as though crushed, "no one can make it go away except the Lord Almighty Himself, man. I gave up drinking to save money, and after that I gave up smoking as well. What else is there for me to give up? My very life? No, I don't blame her. The poor creature's a real thrifty housewife. God is my witness that she's a better person than I am. The fact is that if it weren't for her the street dogs would have had us. But it's the children . . ."

I dived in so as not to seem like the proverbial deaf man at a wedding. "Certainly it seems the children are . . ."

"You can say that again, may He have mercy on your dear departed. The trouble is there's no milk in her breasts, nor yet in the market. What d'you think would happen if the children were to fall ill? If there aren't any medicines in the government hospitals how am I expected to lay my hands on any? So that's how things are with us. Tell me what to do. Give me some solution."

At that moment all appearance of calm drained from his face

and his features took on a look of stark alarm. "Imagine it! She said that was a solution. Good folk, she suggested it as a solution! For sure, either she's gone crazy or I have."

He began slapping at his thighs, which further increased my astonishment and brought the inevitable question to my lips. Then, quite unexpectedly, he gave a tiny nervous laugh which convinced me the man was indeed off his head. "Believe me, there's nothing worse than bottling up one's troubles, man. Keeping silent and cooping it all up has really done for me. For a couple of months I've been living in another world, keeping quiet about what she told me. I'd mull it over this way and that, while I felt like a chicken being roasted over Hell's fire. I was sitting doing my sums for the household expenses, with no clue of what was coming, when she came to me and said, 'Radwan, how's it all going to end?' I said to her, 'God willing, it will turn out all right, Fadwa. I know no more than you do.' She said, 'Radwan, our whole life is one of beggary, and the children are growing up between life and death. The cost of living is killing us—what I mean is, in a word, I want to work.'"

He leaned toward me and there was a strange forlorn look in his eyes. As though he wasn't seeing me, he said, "How should I know? In the beginning I said to her, 'And what about the children, Fadwa?' 'The Provider will look after that,' she said. In order to humor her I said, 'Certainly, He'll look after it, my dear, but what will you work at with that elementary certificate of yours?' 'I'll not work with my certificate,' she said. 'That's all very well,' I told her, '—then with what? Your wits?' Then, more downcast than I'd ever seen her, she said, 'No, Radwan, I'll work. I'll work all right.'"

A yellow pallor clouded his face. I gave up in bewilderment. I uttered not a word, did not even make an attempt to speak. He went on as though in a trance. "To begin with, I didn't want to take it in. If I'd understood what she meant I'd have gone out of my mind. But she left me no escape. She said, 'Radwan, I know it comes as a surprise, and it's tough for you, but it's a fact that our children are hungry and our life is hard. I wanted to tell you just so you wouldn't say I was betraying you. It's been a terrible thing for me, man. Believe me when I tell you that it would be easier for me to lose my four children.' But I said to myself, 'Keep patient, Radwan. Give and take with her a bit—talk it over.' In fact, I started to talk to her, and she talked back. All night long we didn't stop talking and crying. You'd think something awful had happened to us! Some ghastly calamity! By God, I simply don't know! When morning came she was hugging me and crying and I was hugging her and crying. However, to cut a long story short, there was nothing to be done. After that, to tell you the truth, I gave the matter a lot of thought. I told myself that I should inform her family. But her family didn't recognize her at all because she'd fallen in love with me and we'd eloped. And what should I tell my friends? What would they do but spread the story? Even to divorce her didn't make any sense. Where would I park the four children? And where would I find the money for the price of a second wife? And who's to know what she'd be like? I won't hide it from you—I thought of killing her. Just for a second I thought of it, then I laughed at my madness. What wrong had the children done for me to cast myself into prison and them into the street? And what wrong had she done for her to die unjustly? Yes, unjustly, because—God is my witness—all the years we were together she was like a golden lira. If she hadn't been, she wouldn't have told me about it at all."

He wiped the saliva from his mouth with the back of his hand. I was silently engrossed in what he was saying.

"I kept quiet about it, telling myself that, like a summer cloud, it would pass, and I went back to trying to talk to her about it. 'Would you be unfaithful to me, Fadwa?' 'No, Radwan,' she told me. 'Don't make a mistake. If I'd fallen for someone else and gone with him without your knowing, then I'd really have been unfaithful. But I've got nobody but you in the whole world, Radwan, and you know it. I want to work just so we can eat, Radwan.' Imagine it, she said to me, 'And what do we lose, Radwan? I'd close my eyes and imagine it was you with me. It would be just a moment and afterward we'd live like decent folk.' Brother, her idea drove me out of my wits. I was shattered. God curse poverty and the life it brings!"

His voice was choked with tears as his words spattered against the window. I tried to say something, but my tongue stuck inside my mouth as the mud houses of al-Qastal slipped past the glass of the window.

"D'you know what happened after that?" he asked a moment later in a quaking voice.

"What happened?" I asked eagerly.

The driver's assistant called out, "Come on, lads, and hurry up, anyone who's getting off here. It's not a regular stop."

Radwan and some of the passengers rose to their feet. He was interrupted by the question in my eyes and he muttered something amid the din that I did not catch as he hurried to get off. I moved toward the window and saw him making his way toward another passenger, his hand gesticulating from side to side and thumping his chest, then gesturing toward his head, as an expression of bemusement settled on the other passenger's face.

The Women's Room

Hana Atia

ehind dilapidated screens that concealed only their breasts they were taking off voluminous *gallabiya*s that clung to their bodies. The long room heaved with the pungent smell of salt and iodine. In hurried confusion they began exchanging things for makeup, towels, and the one and only mirror. I was getting out of my swimming costume and felt agitated and embarrassed. I began quickly changing my clothes inside one of the cubicles. All at once she was in front of me, crowding me out in the narrow space. Without a word she started taking off her gown, while I waited for her to finish as I wrapped my body round with my towel and stared down at the ground.

I heard her laugh. When I looked up she was undoing her bra and taking out from the left cup a rolled up piece of cloth. Running her hand over the empty place, she said, "My God, it's as if it's still alive and well!"

She began to scrutinize me and smile. I felt my limbs stiffening as I stared and then pointed at that emptiness. "Was it long ago that . . . ?"

"Two years ago." She then took hold of the piece of cloth and said, "At times it seems to move just like it used to—and it feels warm."

Slowly and absentmindedly, she began drying her body as she looked sideways at me. In confusion I fixed the towel around my breasts.

"Shy of me?" she said.

"Not at all."

"Why don't you undress?"

"I was waiting till I got a bit drier."

She took out another bra and a dry piece of cloth from a plastic bag. She started rolling it up and stuffing it into the left cup, then altering it and rolling it up again. Pointing first at the right breast then at the left, she said, "Are they the same?"

"Yes."

"No, see whether it's rounded."

She took out the piece of cloth and rearranged it. I saw her wide eyes and the traces of kohl still showing despite the many hours she had spent in the water.

"Give it to me—I'll do it," I said.

When I took it to roll it up, she pointed at herself and said, "Look what the sea's done! The sea's a cure for everything. This disease will never come back."

As I began lifting up the bra a bit to push in the piece of cloth, I felt a slight dizziness and trembling in my body, and I heard her saying, "Thanks, God keep you safe. My husband says to me, 'By the Prophet, I don't feel any difference. One or two—the one that's there makes up for the other.'"

Pointing at the two, I said, "The one's just like the other, isn't it?"

She passed her hand over them both, then said as she searched about in her plastic bag, "Where's my mirror?"

She produced a small mirror whose surface was soiled by dust-colored spots surrounded by a few clear spaces.

"I'll hold it for you," I told her.

Then we changed places so that the light infiltrating through the high-up apertures in the cubicles would reach her.

"It's almost time for sunset prayers."

"Yes, hurry up and fix them."

"The left one was always smaller than the right. I want them to be just as they used to be."

She went on rearranging the way the piece of cloth was rolled, while remarking, "It's night. It's night and my husband's waiting for me by the sea. You, too, get your clothes on."

Turning my back to her, I quickly took away the towel, almost tripping over it as I did up the bra. I felt her hands on my back, taking hold of the clasp and closing it without a word. At the same speed, I began getting into my clothes, both of us silent. I observed the last thread of orange light making its escape through the aperture. When I turned to her, she appeared quiet and serene.

Passing her hand over herself, she said, "See." We both smiled and she went on, "It's just right."

"Yes."

She put on a black *gallabiya* with red and green flowers. We got ready to leave; the world was gray. I saw her hastening joyfully in the direction of the sea.

It Happened Secretly

Amina Zaydan

Everything was gleaming in a rich redness that issued from the flame of the solitary, enormous candle. The half-empty bottle of vodka that looked, with its streamlined shape after the long pillar of its neck, like a compressed globe, with the translucent, blazing liquor, like a live ember exposed to the air that causes it to burn more fiercely, dancing inside it. The same was true of the half-filled glass, which was closer to the candle, on whose sides jutted drops of wax that had no sooner solidified than they began to glow again, following a fresh drop, inflated like a liquid bubble. How beautifully frightening it was alongside the joyous, mature face. He has drawn near to the candle, the bottle, and the glass, on the outer surface of which are nacreous drops of water, their sparkle reflected in his cheerful, blazing eyes as though they had been hewn from some volcanic mountain. Thus the whole face was shown: the baldness that reached back to above the ears, the matted white hair covering his ears and the sides of his neck, his beard and the prominent cheekbones. It was a happy, childlike face on which contradictions found visible expression, revealing their eternal presence, as though he were reverting back with his soul from the end of his eighty years to the beginning of his years of opening up, this face that has protruded from the darkness and swam and bathed itself so as to be cleansed by the incandescence of the candle and sensuously take into its embrace the half-empty bottle of vodka and the half-filled glass. Behind him stand two men holding billiard cues; they look at him as though they were going to take him off to his final place of rest—but how could such a man cease to exist!

"It's enough for me to see this picture and to touch its colors with the tips of my fingers, to smell it, for a sensation of warmth to flow through me," she said, moving her senses across the oil painting in its white, glassless frame. Small lamps filled the corners with light. Directly behind her, he pressed the light switch and turned it off until she reached the corridor leading to two closed rooms. She pressed the final light switch. She looked at him, meeting head-on his face and thick mustache that covered and hid his upper lip. While avoiding touching him, she said laughing, "It seems that all roads lead to the bedrooms."

From the moment they passed through the front door to the flat it was as though they were crossing into another world, a world able to contain her fear. Recovering her breath, she cast aside the feelings of choking and suffocation she had experienced going up the stairs. She had tried to count them in order to disperse her fear and apprehension, which accompanied the tread of her high heels. She braced herself against the pain in her feet so as not to make a sound as they touched the marble stairs. Even her mind, during the time she was climbing the five flights, could not bear to think beyond standing in front of the wooden door and passing through it. However, all these sensations collapsed and fell stricken to the ground when her hand closed the door and she was enclosed in the flat with its warmth and its colors, so homogenous to her eyes: the rain-white, the blue, and the sandy yellow. Resting her shoulders against the door, she had turned her head like someone waking up from the unconsciousness of cholera. She was met by the African features of her face reflected in the mirror, flushed from the effect of holding her breath as she went up the five flights; also, behind her face, were reflected a number of wooden shelves, on which were ranged collections of poetry. "Nizar . . . Nizar . . . Nizar . . . al-Shinnawi . . . Dante . . . ," she read as she looked them over, moving the books with the tip of her index finger.

He motioned her to enter the living room. She had, however, moved aside the curtaining made of metal strips of colored circles and squares to find herself in the kitchen. She went through another door, where she faced the two closed bedrooms. Putting his arms around her shoulders, he said, "Rania's room—and this is my bedroom."

She went up two steps covered in blue carpeting and crossed through a low, narrow archway that opened onto the living room, which contained two couches and three large armchairs with bulky cushions. She came to a stop in the middle of the room and looked around at the paintings.

"Do you feel safe living among them?" she said. "Aren't you frightened they'll come out of their frames one day? They almost speak out and confirm that they'll come alive."

He was standing by her, contemplating them as though in the company of a child at a display of toys. It pleased him when she seated herself on the sofa facing the dining room, placing the soft blue cushion on her rounded knees, then resting her elbows on the cushion. He was excited by the sight of her clasping her fingers under her chin, and he let his gaze fall on her body, observing its curves and contours as he searched for a way to come to terms with her.

"It's the first time I've been in a house that doesn't have a woman in it," she said.

"That's the best thing about it," he said, turning his head as though following the flight of a fly, for he did not miss the presence of a woman, other than that of his daughter, who was being brought up by her grandmother.

"How do you live," she said, "without a woman chattering away and filling the rooms with her bustle?"

"I can fill the house with them in minutes."

"The smell of a house is different when there's a woman about."

"In every corner of the house I breathe in the smell of them. I made love to a woman against the door of the flat and to another beside the stove so that boiling drops of tea were falling on us. The world is never short of them." Then he added, "And another one insisted on lying on the dining room table. Only a few were patient enough to wait before going into the bedroom—although all roads lead to it. . . . I have known around three hundred women, and they were all virtuous wives and society ladies."

"I am with the two of you, listening and seeing." She laughed a lot as she repeated this phrase written on a marble slab placed above a piece of furniture in the shape of a black hut with several openings for video equipment, television, and a turntable. She got to her feet and rummaged through the records. She took one out of its sleeve.

"Do you mind?" she asked as she put it on.

"Not at all, just as you like. I haven't listened to a single record since I brought them from Russia in the seventies."

She stamped her foot on the floor covered in blue carpeting before the record moved under the needle. She went on looking at the Russian paintings until she stopped at the picture of the old man and the vodka—as she had named it.

"Why did you travel to Russia?"

"I was on a training course for a year."

"Training for what?"

"For war."

She looked at him. "Then you fought in '73?"

"And in Yemen and in '67."

"In what branch?"

"Infantry—I was a sniper."

"Then you're a retired sniper—you live with the eye and heart of a sniper."

"Yes, I had thought that I would wake up in the middle of the day and be freed of this mold in which the military had cast me, but I found myself clinging to the mold and burying myself further still in its shell."

"Did you kill anyone?"

"Yes, many are the heads I've cropped."

"Do you remember the first one?"

"Are we going to spend the time talking?" he said, coming up to her and trying to embrace her from behind after she had put on the light in front of the last picture in the corridor leading to the bedroom.

Like some mythical creature, he gathered himself together and gazed at a world lit up by light switches. The darkness retreated, defining the universe. Pelted onto its surface were dots of colored lights from the ships lying in the Canal. She stared at them until the lights danced before her eyes. She breathed in deeply the odor of washed buildings and of the earth moist with drops of rain and that of waves crashing against the walls of the Canal.

The air was saturated with these smells and her senses gulped down this strong mixture, breath by breath.

"From here you can see the spit of the Canal, the gulf, and

the eastern shore, and from the kitchen window the whole of the Ataqa mountain. When the sun first falls on it, it appears golden, later silver, and finally it tucks itself up for the night. You live wholly in the heart of things," she said, elated, as her words danced in the empty space before her. She would have liked to cast aside the abstinence of her thirty-nine years alongside her shoes, and set off at a run to catch up with what remained to her of her life as a woman.

A gust of cold air struck against her and she closed the glass window. Gazing out, it was as if the light of a candle were dancing on the darkness of the glass surface. She let down the blind of metal-blue matting.

The smoke curled up in endless, eddying circles from the earthenware mugs of tea. He placed the tin tray on the rectangular table, whose glass surface was buried under a motley collection of crystal ashtrays, china vases, and albums of color photographs. Flipping through the pictures, which were all of his daughter in bathing costume, in school uniform, in a speckled, sand-colored uniform like that worn by commando shock troops, or of her dancing and holding a baton, she said, "It seems you're enthralled by your daughter."

"She's all that is left of me."

"In addition to the medals and the records and the oil paintings—and the smell of women."

He turned away his head as though he were avoiding a strong smell when his eye alighted on a picture in which a blonde woman was standing beside his daughter, a woman of a strong, unquenchable beauty.

"This is your wife—she's beautiful. So why did you divorce her?"

"I'll never go into that," he said, gathering up the albums from her lap and closing them.

"But she doesn't look like her daughter," she said, casting a look at the final picture.

He had gone back to regarding the picture in silence, searching for lost aspects of similarity between the girl and her mother. Then he brought the two covers of the album together with a resounding bang.

"Where is she now?"

"She lives with her mother's mother."

"I mean your wife—the one you divorced."

"In Abu Dhabi."

"And what does she do in Abu Dhabi?"

"She works."

"As a teacher?"

"No."

"What does she do, then?"

"I don't know and I'm not interested to know."

"Why are you upset?"

"I don't want to talk about her."

"Does she frighten you so much?"

He looked at her with alert, reddened eyes. He closed them and rubbed his eyelids with his fingertips.

Through her cold nostrils a warmth permeated to her limbs. Her feeling of excitement calmed down. Smoke rose up gently and was dispersed in the empty space. He held out his lighted cigarette to her. The white smoke left her mouth in a thick cloud. There clung to her throat a feeling of bitterness she had first tasted with Sumayya, her cousin, in the laundry room on the rooftop when she had sneaked a cigarette and had believed that the bitterness was a punishment for her; thus this bitterness was forever mixed up with feelings of guilt.

Coming close to her, he passed the tip of his tongue over her lips, savoring the taste of sweetened tea and the bitterness of the cigarette. She saw the abstinence of her thirty-nine years lying beside her shoes. Without resistance or argument, she yielded without any sense of regret; she embraced his kiss as though it were the first religion vouchsafed to her.

He put back the glass of tea and the cigarette, then took up her glass and let her rise to her feet to fiddle around in the drawers of the black wooden cave: cassettes, sex films and films of private parties, obscene china and ivory figurines of naked women and black men, and miniature cedar trees and date palms.

She opened the crystal glass of the cupboard opposite the dining table. His medals and badges were scattered over the shelves under a thin layer of dust.

"Why did you fight?" she asked.

"Duty."

"Duty for the sake of duty . . ."

She took hold of a metal plaque inscribed in gold lettering.

"Major-General Mohamed Hamza . . . who's this Mohamed Hamza?"

"My brother."

"So the family's full of fighters—no scholars and no thinkers."

"In war the brain doesn't operate, in fact it is done away with when faced by duty."

"Don't say duty, rather say that war is a legacy that one inherits."

"This brother of mine is in charge of a governorate with a million people."

"And why didn't you become a governor?"

"What I did in the war was the equal of being twenty governors."

"You fight and you govern and you make love and you make sons who are copies of yourselves and dance to your history—all alike. Time retrogresses."

"You won't understand the life of a fighter unless you your-self have fought. You won't realize what it means for me to return from the front. I divest myself of my authority with my military uniform, just as I discard the role of leader alongside the bed. I leave it to my wife to lead me to it, which is when I know that there is another man who leads her there." She tried not to show sympathy for the distracted intonations of his voice.

"It seems," she said, "that the fighting man is a sadist in war-fare and a masochist in bed. And in governing? How do you think he is in governing?"

"Of necessity he'll be all of that together."

From two silver swords crossed at the middle came a reflection of light that struck at her eyes. The small medal, laid out inside the box lined outside with blue velvet and inside with white satin, was shiny despite the scattered grains of dust.

The picture of her husband swung in front of her like a pen-dulum. She saw him half-naked, half-covered with his white shroud as though she had listened to the early morning sounds that remind her of him: the crowing of cocks, the fluttering of sparrows' wings above the bedewed eucalyptus tree. She came to, as though a long, rattling scream had burst out of her chest and throat.

She closed the glass and collapsed beside him like a dried seed of three thousand years slipping down toward a pool of water.

With her husband's death she had realized that there was no longer time for the sensation of pain. She had gathered up his framed photographs and belongings and crammed them into an old box, which she had placed at the bottom of a chest that would be forever closed. She had not spoken about him to her two daughters. She had buried his memory in the same way he himself had been buried, just as the fence with which he had

193

encircled her had become tattered and torn. He no longer came to the house with folded newspaper and empty mind, searching around in the boxes of condiments, counting the bags of meat and chicken, handling the childhood of his daughters with such severity, and examining her clothes before she went out to make sure no hair had slipped from her headcloth and that her dress was long enough. She had been freed from all that, though her awareness of this freedom had become narrowly circumscribed during the ten years since his death, for she had not known the ways in which her freedom could be utilized.

"Am I now exercising my freedom?" she inquired of herself in astonishment.

"This is your natural right in life—to live in the manner that pleases you."

He imagined that it was the years of being a widow that had thrown her at him. He was not aware that her sense of time, which appeared on the whole faster than his own, broken up as it was into moments and days, was what had made her cling to him. She had been doubtful whether he was the sort that would truly please her. Always she yearned for a real shaking-up when, waking as usual, she would find the boundaries of her city had become too restricted for her and that she was no longer in harmony with her two daughters, her surroundings, and her family. So she stands outside her house as she sells it and receives the money after loading her necessities into a large, antiquated car, when everything around her appears chaotic, even her way of dressing, her hair, and her things piled up behind the car, with her two daughters leaping about around her. Then the moment swallowed up this picture she was describing to him as though she were recounting to him some crucial dream, as one of his hands undid the large buttons on her dress and the other passed over her face and lips.

They were like two hedgehogs clutching each other, and they remained like that, so that each could not but harm the other. He was harmed by the essence of his own weakness, while she was harmed by her feeling that she had brought him to this weakness. She turned to him as she was opening the door of his flat, at the moment when he raised his face to her so that they might say together, "What has happened today must remain a secret."

Whiteness of Silver

Abdullah Bakhshaween

I n front of the door of the building he stopped me with a gesture from the stick he was supporting himself on without inclining his body. He was thin and about the age of my father, who had departed this world before I had moved to this building.

"You're the new tenant?" he inquired. "What's your name?"

It was after midday prayers on an extremely hot day, and I was in a hurry to pass. I told him my name.

"The son of whom?" he asked, smiling.

I mentioned my father's name and surname.

"How wonderful!" He said it as though he knew him well, while at the same time the faraway look in his eyes suggested that he was searching in his memory in vain for the owner of the name. Coming out of his distraction, he said, "Where is he? I want to say hello to him."

I was taken aback by his question. Wishing to rid myself of him, I said, "He's at the mosque; he hasn't returned from midday prayers yet."

"Give him my regards," he said, about to go up the stairs. "Tell him: Uncle Jaber sends you his regards. Don't forget." And before I had moved away he said, "Tell him I'll pay him a visit soon."

I stood amazed at myself, not knowing what had prompted me to lie to the old man, who had begun to go up the steps, as he went on repeating, "A blessed dwelling . . . a blessed dwelling."

I made my way to my car, rebuking myself, though without any feeling of guilt, for the situation ended there with each of us going his own way.

Three months had passed since I had received news of my father's death. I had not been able to cast a final look at him, nor to walk in his funeral procession, because news of his death had reached me only several hours before his burial; I had been far away and would not have been able to get there until everything was over.

I had been overcome by sadness and anger when I realized that I would arrive only in time to accept people's condolences. I told myself that the man who had looked after his burial would receive the condolences, and that there was no point in my going there to dwell on a grief whose sincerity God alone knew.

This did not mean that I did not love my father; it was more that I did not want anyone to see the extent of my distress at his death.

I was in the habit of waking up early. I would get up to take my wife and children to their schools and would then return to go to sleep again, not waking up a second time until after the call to midday prayers had been given, at the time they came home. Despite the fact that I go out at the same time almost every day, I nevertheless do not usually come across any of the neighbors. Thus the meeting with the old man threw me into confusion when I inexcusably lied to him.

197

I began to blame myself, being unhappy for the strange manner in which I had lied to him about my father's death. Yet the matter remains ambiguous inside me, for I do not possess any absolute certainty that confirms his death other than that quick conversation in which the person pretended to know nothing about how he had died and began telling me about the time for the burial, which he knew I would not be able to attend.

On many a night, when overtaken by feelings of nostalgia, I continue to think about my father and converse with him, when it occurs to me that he might possibly not have died.

The last time I saw him was on the day when I was due to travel and we went off to say goodbye to him. We looked for him in one of the cafés where he usually sat among a number of his contemporaries watching the group who play dominoes. They all turned around when our car came to a stop. My father jumped to his feet joyfully. Kissing his hand and head, I said, "We're going away."

Resignedly he said, "May you have a safe journey, God willing," then he went off to the children and began playing with them, evading their persistent question, "When will you be coming to see us, Grandpa?"

After that farewell devoid of sorrow, with the promise that he would come to see us in a week, we departed. But three days later there came that calamitous telephone call informing me of the time of the burial.

It was not long before I had forgotten the old man as I became engrossed in my work, which begins after the sunset prayer until late into the night.

The following day I woke to persistent ringing at the front door. I looked at the clock fixed to the wall in front of me: it pointed to eleven in the morning.

I got up in a state of confusion, for I was not accustomed to receiving anyone at such an hour. When I opened the door I was taken aback by his disheveled hair, which looked like my father's; he was in his house clothes, not smartly dressed as I had found him on the first occasion. He bore a close resemblance to my father, in that way that all old people resemble each other.

I stepped back in trepidation as I asked with surprise, "Welcome, uncle. What do you want?"

"Peace be upon you and the mercy of God and His blessings," he said, smiling and ignoring my question.

"Upon you be peace," I said, my astonishment still there. "I hope everything's all right?"

"Is he at home?"

"Who?" I asked in embarrassment.

"Your father," he said, retaining his smile.

I took hold of myself, recalling yesterday's meeting, and said, hard pressed, "No, he's gone out."

"Where's he gone?" he said in surprise. "It's not prayer time yet."

"Sometimes he sits at the shopkeeper's opposite the mosque," I said hurriedly, "and doesn't return till after the prayers."

His smile vanished all at once, his features changed, and his face became filled with a strange air of distress and disappointment. "What a pity," he said. "I thought he was at home. I thought I'd come to say hello to him, that we might chat for a while, and then go off to prayers together."

I was overwhelmed by a feeling of regret.

I had not believed that that slip of the tongue could lead me to such a distressing situation. I wanted to apologize to him for what I had said, words that he had taken seriously; I wanted to tell him that my father had died several months ago without my attending his funeral or being there when he died, and that a part

199

of me does not want to believe the story of his death, which had come to me by way of a hasty telephone conversation. But, instead of that, I heard myself saying apologetically, "If he'd known you'd be coming he would certainly have waited for you."

"Didn't you tell him you'd met me?"

"Yes, I did," I answered spontaneously.

"But you didn't tell him that I'd be paying him a visit shortly," he said, as though apologizing on my behalf. "That's due to the hastiness of youth, is it not?"

"Things on my mind . . . worries," I said, dodging the question.

He was standing in dejected thought, his eyes filled with words the size of his whole life that had gone by, while I had an intractable pain twinging in my side that shattered into pieces by his feet after he had turned around and was about to climb the stairs. All at once he came to a stop and said in farewell, "Don't forget to inform him that I came and didn't find him."

I don't know what I replied at the time, but I stood as though pinned to the door until he had mounted the stairs opposite my door and disappeared from sight.

After that I tried to go back to sleep but could not. The image of him standing at the door, disheveled and as thin as a ghost, came back to harass me. I was violently shaken by regret, which made me berate myself harshly, a feeling accompanied by agonizing distress. How had I placed myself in such an extraordinary situation? Where, I wondered, had my feelings at the loss of my father led me?

For long nights my wife would sit silently watching me as I sat grave-faced beside her thinking about the news of his death that had reached me in the way it had. She would occasionally interrupt our silence and, attempting not to upset me, would say, "Make the journey and find out for yourself."

I would stare at her with defeated eyes then say angrily, "If he did actually die, I'll kill one of them, and if he didn't I'll also do it . . . . Let me be, please."

She would say in protest, "Are you going to go on mulling it over and killing yourself with apprehensions and misgivings?"

The days went by, however, and I remained undecided, not wanting to travel to make sure and yet unwilling to resign myself to his death. Thus his presence, with that joyful air of his at the moment we said farewell, continued to dominate my imagination.

Had I discharged upon the old man the thoughts that my inner mind had been surreptitiously suggesting to me, to the point that I lied without imagining that he would come and knock at my front door to ask about my father with such warmth that I had been thrown into confusion?

Was it that I had been waiting for someone to ask me about my father so that I might address him with just that answer that I had found no difficulty in composing and proclaiming with such unwavering certainty, even after I had recognized the truth that I had lied? Or was it that the sight of the old man had helped me to lie out of pity for him because of the mention of death, as he asked me in a way that was not devoid of cheerfulness?

I no doubt had not wished to upset him by mentioning death.

I felt impotent; I had lost my ability to think at those limits that had made me conceal my misgivings with that extraordinary form of indifference that enfolds me and governs my behavior.

With the beginning of the weekend holiday I take a rest from the burden of waking up early. I sleep right through with the cooperation of my children, who spend the morning of their day off at some place far from the room in which I sleep. They leave me until I wake up after having had my fill of sleep, so that afterward they can propose the manner in which they wish to spend the rest of the day.

On that Thursday they waited for me to wake up so as to talk to me about the guest who had visited them while I was asleep. Sitting on my lap, the youngest, heedless of the others, said, "Papa, my grandfather was here while you were asleep."

Before I was able to collect myself, the middle one said jeeringly, "He's not your grandfather, stupid—he just looks like him!"

I was completely baffled, as my wife stared at me with a knowing look.

She gathered up the children and took them out of the room with the words, "Go and play for a while in your room and don't make Daddy angry with you."

She went back to staring at me inquiringly, as she said, "We had a visited from one of the neighbors—he's an old man the same age as your father. He sat with the children for a while then went off."

Without trying to restrain my fear, I said, "What did he say to them? What did they talk about?"

"I don't know because I wasn't sitting with them. Ask your son—he was the one who met him and talked with him."

My fear was grew as I called out fretfully to my older son. Confused, he stood in front of me as I asked him irritably, "What did the old man ask you about? What did you say to him?"

Gauging my reaction, he said slowly, "He asked me about my grandfather and I told him he wasn't here, that he'd gone away and would be here in a few days. He sat down and played with my brothers for a while, then went away."

I gave a sigh of relief, recalling that in the confusion my feelings had been in I had been careful to hide from my children the news of their grandfather's death, since I was not sure about it.

Noticing that I had relaxed, he said confidently, "He was happy when we called him 'grandpa.' He's a very nice old man."

"Is that everything?" I inquired calmly.

"When we said goodbye," he said casually, "he said he would come to visit us when my grandfather returned from his travels."

The weekend over, my life returned to normal, though one thing was changed: the image of the old man was imprinted on my mind, had penetrated there surreptitiously and now scarcely left me, even though I did not see him for the next three days.

But when the time of day came that he had first knocked at my door before the midday prayer I found myself awake, for I had had the impression of hearing the doorbell. Getting to my feet hastily, I opened the door but found no one. I tried to go back to sleep, but no sooner did I doze off than I woke up with a start at the sound of his voice reaching me as he conversed with someone in the sitting room. I began to be upset by my apprehensions as, in bed at noon, I listened to the sound of non-existent voices. I felt alone and afraid, alone at such an hour of the morning. I heard the sound of my father's laughter issuing from so many places that I became absolutely convinced that he had come back.

I got up hastily and went through the rooms but found nothing except for my children's things strewn about. Despite being happy at the idea that he had gone away, as my children had said, which provided me with an excuse whenever I should meet the old man, I none the less felt embarrassed at having lied to him, and I lived in hope that I would never meet him again.

But, without realizing it, I began, with the passage of time, to feel that I was truly missing him.

At noon that day, I dressed and went down to ask about him. The janitor of the building had the habit of leaving his room and occupying a chair in front of the front door for most of the day. I asked him about the old man, and he told me that he lived with his daughter, her husband, and children in the flat above my own; he did no work during the day but owned a small workshop for polishing silver in the gold market. He sat there every day from the afternoon prayer until the call was given for the sunset prayer. The janitor informed me that they had come to live in the building at almost the same time as I had.

That afternoon I went out to wander about aimlessly, thinking of my father, who had missed by a long way the date he had given the children. I felt angry as I went over the details of that telephone conversation that had so thrown me into confusion.

It was a painful anger, blazing more fiercely with the days and preventing me from going there to bring the truth to light.

My father had been alone for several years after the death of my mother, refusing to live with any of his sons, who had offered, without any great enthusiasm or insistence, that he move in with them.

He had said that if he wanted to live with any of his sons he would live with me, but for the fact that I lived far away and in a place where he knew no one. They therefore left him alone and each went his own way.

He had rented a small shop beside the café in which he was accustomed to sit, a shop in which he sold scarcely anything. He filled it with miscellaneous small articles that he would collect during his rovings in the old quarters, and of which he sold only the brass and the aluminum to buyers who passed by his shop from time to time.

As for the primus stoves, mantle lamps, and lanterns, he would polish and repair them and then hang them up in a prominent place at the shop's entrance, despite the fact that they were little in demand and found no buyers because of the modern substitutes that were available. He would thus leave the shop door open practically the whole time, and would spend all day long in the café with his friends, some of whom had made it their living quarters—my father included, they would take the café chairs to a corner far from the general hubbub and employ them as beds.

I knew that my footsteps would finally lead me to the gold market. Having left behind the shops, I looked around for his store, which lay in an out-of-the-way corner leading off one of the back streets of the market, with nothing separating it from the quarter except for a wide dusty street. He was sitting behind the table on which rested his equipment for polishing silver, holding between his thighs a brass vessel from which emanated the smell of turpentine.

As I greeted him, both his hands were inside the vessel, as he energetically polished it. He raised his head and glanced quickly at me, then went back to examining the inside of the vessel, without paying me any more attention.

I seated myself on the empty chair in front of him and regarded him in silence. From time to time he would extract a golden strip from the vessel and examine it with interest before throwing it into the wastebin.

The color of his fingers when he took them out of the vessel appalled me. I was seeing them for the first time since I'd known him: in contrast to his brown skin that pulsated with life, his fingers were completely white, in a way that made them repulsive, the effect of the turpentine. They were long, thin fingers, whose tips had been eaten away and had become ulcerated. He concealed the pain behind the hard features of his face.

An age seemed to pass as I sat there, the street clamorous

with the sound of boys playing football. Cars drove swiftly by, enveloping us in dust, almost preventing us from drawing breath, while he worked tirelessly at polishing the inside of the vessel, continuing to throw small pieces into the waste-bin without putting any of them aside and without raising his head or addressing me.

He used to leave the mosque each day after afternoon prayers and, during his walk to his store, collect up all the yellow-colored metal objects he could find and throw them into the receptacle filled with turpentine, in which he immersed them for several days. Then, when he had a number of them, he would get down to polishing them, disregarding the effect of that burning chemical substance that was almost eating away his fingers.

The tips of the fingers had become white, the burning solution having penetrated to the living flesh under his nails, which had stiffened and were contorted, thus causing him additional pain—and yet he appeared to be indifferent.

Once a week he would gather up the small pieces that he believed to be gold, tie them up in a small bag, and shyly submit them to one of the gold shop owners. The man would immediately throw them into the street, regarding him in silence.

Before the call to sunset prayers he closed the door of his store and we began our walk in the direction of the house without exchanging a word. It was as though we had not yet learned the power of speech!

With unhurried steps we walked, the old man's hands swinging at his sides and his head hanging down staring at the ground under his feet, either through habit or because of the weight of years, while I clasped my hands behind my back, worried and in a bad mood, words raging in my chest that were bridled and refused to issue forth.

In front of the door of the building I left the old man conversing with the janitor and began climbing the stairs without bidding him farewell.

On the following morning I made up my mind to travel: I would go directly to my father. If I did not find him I would at least find out the truth of the matter and would return without seeing any of them, for I did not know what my reaction would be if I met one of them.

I reached the café around the time for the call to evening prayers. My father's friends were gathering up the chairs from off the sidewalk. When they spotted my car and some of them had recognized me, one of them rushed toward me, his hand held out in greeting. "So, it's you, my son—may God recompense you generously for the loss of your father."

"Then, sir, my father has died?" I said, my hopes rudely dashed.

"He died some time ago—didn't your brothers tell you of his death?"

"I don't know, sir . . . I don't know," I said helplessly.

Sensing my sadness, he took me by the hand toward a secluded corner, as he said affectionately, "Come and sit down, my son . . . . Sit down."

There were no chairs close by, so we sat on the sidewalk.

"Praise God you came," he said happily. "Your father left something with me for you." I looked at him with curiosity as he put his hand into the bag attached to the leather belt round his waist. From it he took out a small purse, which he handed to me. "Now I've cleared myself of the trust your late father left with me," he said with satisfaction.

Without curiosity I opened the purse. It contained the change from some money I had given him before I traveled away, and a silver ring that he used to wear on the ring finger of his right hand. Placing the ring in my pocket, I held out the money to my father's friend. He drew his hand away and said sadly, "I ask God's forgiveness, my son, it wouldn't be right for me to take the deceased's money, and it wouldn't be right for you to take it either—it's for all of you."

Almost in tears, I said to him, "Take it and give it away in charity, for I haven't got the time to do that."

"You can give away your share in charity," he explained, "but what shall I do with your brothers' share?"

"Give it away, too," I told him quickly. "None of them is in need."

My father had died in the café around the time of the call to morning prayers. On the previous day my brothers had visited him and he had appeared indisposed. They had suggested that he go to the hospital but he had refused; perhaps their suggestion had not been particularly insistent. They had sat with him for about an hour and had then gone off with the intention of returning the following day. When he was once again sitting with his friends he appeared tired and preoccupied. Then all at once he had extracted the money from his pocket and had taken the ring from his finger and had asked his friend to keep them for me.

When my brothers appeared on the following day, they saw the ambulance and the police cars. The café owner lost no time in making them known amid the large gathering of people filling the place, before any of them had found out what had happened. He pointed them out to the police officer, who made his way to them, while trying to disperse the crowd. The officer led them toward a cane chair on which he had been laid out. Removing the cover from the face, he asked them, "Is this your father?"

They turned to one another in astonishment before one of them said, "Yes."

The officer regarded them for an instant, then said tersely, "And you left him to die like this?"

He moved away from them as he gave instructions for the body to be removed to the ambulance. He motioned to them to follow him. "Come along to the police station," he said as he was about to get into the police car, "so we can complete the formalities for burial."

At the police station one of them filled in the special form, which the officer hastily signed. He then asked them to proceed to the hospital to take possession of the body. It was afternoon by the time they had contacted me to say that prayers were to be said over him and that he was to be buried late that afternoon.

Having learned the details of what had happened, I drove back to where I had come from. Outside the city I stopped at a filling station. After filling up the tank, I drove off for a distance, then stopped at the side of the road, hardly able to see. I sat down on the ground, my back resting against the car, and began to sob. I continued weeping loudly, my whole being convulsed.

I woke up in the afternoon, tired and distressed. I dressed hastily and set off for the old man's shop. Behind the table for polishing the silver he was hugging a pot between his thighs and working on it. It was as though I were seeing him for the first time. I came to a stop opposite him and looked at the shop, which was empty except for that small table, upon which were stacked those small and simple pieces of equipment, without a solitary piece of silver.

I sat down opposite him and asked, "Where's the silver you polish, sir?"

His hands ceased their working and he regarded me gravely as he smiled.

"These days," he said, embarrassed, "no one uses silver for decoration."

His embarrassment confused me. I felt a stab of regret at having made him explain things in a way that had made him uncomfortable.

He went back to bending over the vessel and working hard at it. It was immediately apparent that the quick movement of his hands inside the pot of turpentine had awakened much of the pain he was unable to curb. This could be seen from the convulsions of his face as he stubbornly fought against the pain, though without taking his fingers from the pot, as though it were some punishment he had imposed on himself. All the time I had my eyes glued to his face, at a loss as to what to do.

Then, all at once, as though against his will, he withdrew his hands from the vessel and placed them inside a pot of cold water to stifle the fire that blazed in them. After a while he began contemplating the whiteness of his fingers, which he held far apart before the pain forced him to raise them up high. Placing his hands on his head, he began to moan.

The Return of the Prisoner

Buthayna al-Nasiri

A bove all else, the house he returned to was not his house, the woman not his wife, nor yet the children his sons.

The car took him to a two-storied house painted white and surrounded by a spacious garden in a quarter on the city outskirts he had never been to before.

Inside was a thin woman. The veins in her neck twitched nervously and her forehead wrinkled into a frown that the smile she greeted him with did not succeed in removing. She rushed toward him when he first placed his foot inside the house, then it was as though something had curbed her exuberance so that she came to a stop and extended her hand.

As for the children, they sat pinned with embarrassment to the couches in the living room, seemingly forced to keep silent and well-behaved, as though in the presence of a guest who would shortly be leaving. He knew three of them, though he now had to recall their names and to make sure who was who. As for the fourth, the youngest, he had not previously met him and did not even know his name, for he had left the mother when she was pregnant with him ten years ago.

They began to get acquainted through his general questions and their brief answers, and they ended up in a solemn silence that hung over their heads.

Unable to raise his eyes to her face, he asked the woman, "When did you buy the house?"

Even her voice had changed, had become harsher, as she said, "We didn't buy it already built. I put it up bit by bit. I sold the old one, borrowed from the bank, and supervised the workmen myself. It was a difficult time, what with the responsibility of bringing up four boys."

"You've done a great job," he told her, staring at the walls and ceiling.

"I paid off the final installment of the loan last year," she said.

"It never occurred to me that you'd be able to stand on your own two feet. The woman I remember used to rely on me for everything. I would think of you all when I was there and this feeling would torment me."

"It was a hard time—ten years is quite a while."

"It is."

"And the days change one."

"They do."

"Would you like to see over the house?" she asked eagerly.

"As you like."

The bedroom furniture was the one thing that had not changed, and he found it familiar. There was the wardrobe with the four doors and the wooden top carved with flowers and birds, and the dressing table with the square mirror which he was now standing in front of; the face he now saw in this mirror was not the one he had seen there ten years ago. He had grown thinner,

212

the bones of his face had become more prominent, his hair had grown white, and his shoulders were bowed from the sorrows that had added years to his actual age.

When it was time to sleep, the bed was the same one that had united their dreams in past times and that he had always dreamed he would sleep in again, but the woman and the man were strangers. He was careful not to touch her body as he sank into his side of the comfortable bed and he felt her keeping herself at a distance. He stared at the ceiling lit by moonbeams that came through the window and his thoughts began floating off thousands of miles away, crossing the borders to the prison camp. He saw the faces of those of his comrades who were still alive; he imagined them spread out on the ground, sunk in a heavy sleep after the hardships of the waking day, fleeting smiles on their faces as they dreamed of returning home.

The iron gates clang suddenly and the guards yell roughly at them, "Get up!" They awake from their dreams to find themselves being herded with sticks into the camp courtyard. He crouches in the long file, his hands on top of his head. An officer whose face cannot be seen walks along between them. He talks in a monotonous tone. "Your country has let you down. You are here with us till you rot." The sun's rays grow more scorchingly hot. He feels cramp in his arms and legs, a dryness in his throat. He will not be able to bear it another second. He falls to the ground. The guards hurl themselves at him with their sticks; he is dragged along the ground by his hands until his arms are almost wrenched from their sockets. The door of a tomb-like cell is thrown open and he is pitched into it. The door is shut with a clang that rings in his brain. He raises his head to find that the ceiling allows him to sit only in a crouched position. He curls up in the dark, letting out a continuous moaning like a wounded animal.

213

He hears his name being repeated insistently. He opens his eyes wide in the darkness. Then, suddenly, a glaring light floods the place and he closes his eyelids in pain.

"Are you all right?"

"What happened?"

"You were moaning."

"I was dreaming."

He moves his dry tongue around in his mouth. "Can I have something to drink?"

The woman brings him a glass of water, which he gulps down, then he leans against the back of the bed. He no longer feels any desire to sleep.

"Can you imagine—when I was there I used to dream of the house each night, and now I'm here and in my own bed I dream of the camp? It seems the suffering isn't over yet."

"If you'd like to talk I'm listening."

"I wanted to ask you why you didn't send me a card or a letter all those years."

"We didn't know you were still alive."

"Why didn't you try to find out through the Red Cross, as everyone does?"

"I tried in the beginning and I was told that your name wasn't registered with them."

"If you'd made more of an effort," he said sharply, "you'd have known how to find me, but you all abandoned me."

"It's not for you to blame me," she replied, her voice raised. "The circumstances were difficult and I had enough troubles of my own. Everybody regarded you as missing."

"It's clear that my reappearance isn't welcome, for here you are raising your voice at me, and the children don't even know me. You didn't have the time to talk to them about me. You were busy building houses. What was wrong with our old house?"

She got up from the bed, saying firmly, "I'm not going to answer you."

She left the room, slamming the door after her.

He looked about him like someone who had been locked up, feeling that the walls were narrowing and the roof descending so that he was unable to raise his head. He curled up on the bed, filled with the sensation that he had not left his imprisonment and that everything around him was unreal. It was as though he were watching a never-ending nightmare: a vast house that almost encompassed him, children who were strangers to him, and a woman toward whom he could not extend even a finger.

With the morning light he crept out, careful not to make a sound. He went out to the garden. He shook the branch of a nearby tree and the dew was scattered over his face and clothes. Happening to turn to one side, he saw the youngest of his sons sitting on the steps leading to the house. He was holding his head in the palms of his hands, immersed in thought or sadness.

He seated himself beside him, and the boy looked as if he had been taken by surprise. He moved slightly away from the man, who asked him, "What are you doing here at this early hour?"

"I was thinking."

"Shouldn't you be going to school?"

"I don't want to go to school today."

"Then you don't have to go. I too want to spend some time with you all so I can get to know you better."

"But I don't want to go for another reason."

"It must be a really good reason. Can you tell me it?"

"Because of my friend."

"What did he do?"

"He's our neighbor too and he's bound to know you've come back, and he'll tell everybody in the school."

"And what's wrong with that? What's that got to do with wanting to stay away?"

The boy lowered his head and muttered, "Because they all believe you died a hero's death ten years ago."

This surprising news silenced him. After remaining quiet for a long time he asked, "Was it you who told them that? What's wrong in being a prisoner-of-war?"

The boy kept silent.

"Would you prefer it if I were dead?"

The boy burst forth, talking loudly and fast, as though repeating some lesson he had learned by heart: "My friends say that heroes die defending their countries. But a prisoner is a coward who has surrendered so he can stay alive."

He caught his breath, then said, "In real wars things aren't always quite like that. Not every prisoner has surrendered because he is a coward. There may be some mistake in his commander's plan, or the ammunition has run out, or perhaps the enemy's numbers were greater than expected."

The boy gave a shrug of his shoulders and said, "I wanted you to go on being a hero in the eyes of my friends. How can I show them my face after today?"

"You'd prefer I were dead?" He shook his head, not believing what his ears had heard. His feelings of bitterness and despair grew.

Here was the youngest of his sons wishing, perhaps deep down, that he had not come back, that he had stayed on as a prisoner, completely forgotten, lest his return should embarrass him in front of his friends. What was he to do? Should he seek out some war in which to fight until he was killed? Suddenly he got to his feet as though he had made up his mind about something and went up the steps to the kitchen door. His eyes met those of his wife, who had been standing in the doorway. He understood from the way she looked at him that she had been listening to the conversation, which only increased his sensation of shame and the feeling that he was not wanted in this house. He crossed the kitchen with resolute steps to the living room and from there went upstairs to the bedroom.

—He got up from beside his son and moved to the kitchen. His eyes met mine in a look that seemed to me to be full of reproach and blame. Then he made his way through the kitchen and went up the stairs to the bedroom. I said to myself, "Let's leave him to calm down and get back to normal." The children had gone to school, all except for the little one. After that I busied myself with preparing lunch and didn't notice anything untoward. When the children returned we set the table and sat down as usual to eat. We didn't miss him until my elder son said, "Where is he?"

He didn't say "my father." I asked him to go and call him. After a while he returned to say that no one was answering from behind the closed door. It was then that I felt really alarmed and the thought occurred to me—I don't know why—that he had done something to himself, for ever since he had been back he hadn't been normal. I rushed upstairs, followed by the children. I pushed open the door to find myself in an empty room.

"Where's your father, children?"

"Perhaps he's in the bathroom."

One of them went to the bathroom but he wasn't there.

"Where's your father, children?" I repeated the question.

"The case he brought with him has disappeared," said the oldest.

"Perhaps he went back to where he came from," said the young one.

One of them rebuffed him with the words, "Shut up, you idiot!"

*

217

—He got up from beside me, shaking his head. My mother was standing by the kitchen door. She stood aside for him and he disappeared inside.

After some moments I went in after him. He was nowhere to be found. I went to my room and took out my magazines I had read time and again and began flipping through the pages, having nothing else to do. After a while I heard the sound of footsteps pacing up and down in the upstairs room, then they stopped for a time, so I imagined he'd sat down or gone to sleep on the bed. But some time later I heard something like the sound of footsteps creeping down the stairs.

I opened the door slightly and began following him with one eye as he descended the stairs carrying the small suitcase he'd brought with him yesterday. He hung about for a time near the kitchen, then slipped out of the back door. I walked behind him at a quick pace, keeping close to the wall. From an opening in the garden gate I saw him standing uncertainly in the middle of the road looking to right and left. Then, giving the suitcase a shake, as though arriving at a decision, he walked to the right in the direction of the main road. I continued to follow him with my gaze as he moved away, that thin man with the graying hair and bowed back who had come to us yesterday evening and had spent the night in our house and who had talked to me for a while this morning. I continued to watch him until he had disappeared from sight.

A Boat on the Water

Said al-Kafrawi

H e had the sensation of being threatened by danger from
every side. From between his hideout and the fort high
above a hill overlooking the water that he would never
reach in the time he was destined to live, their voices carried to
him with their ringing laughter in the silent emptiness that was
sundered from time to time by gunfire.

(You should have come from the south.)

If he raised himself on tiptoe he was able to see them standing by the opening in the rock. He was afraid they would close
in on him from in front and behind—those men who do not stop
laughing and chatting away the night—and they would encompass him.

(What concerns me is reaching the boat.)

His fear grew that, alone in this desert land, he was facing his
entire life, which had become wholly a moment of flight.

(The boat.)

He again looks around behind him.

They were there. He sees their khaki uniforms, their glinting weapons. The odor of the sea is wafted to him with that of musty blood and the salt-flats that resemble deep-red roses spread out as far as the eye can see, stagnant and motionless, and the desert plants, coarse and prickly, and the yellow sands embellished with the abandoned huts of fishermen, and the day hurtling toward the western reaches of the sun, dyeing the earth the color of sunset.

He grew alert at the sight of the soldiers moving away from the bridge. He felt a certain sense of peace stealing into his consciousness and found himself whispering, "Now the coast is clear." He reckoned that he could cut through behind the hill, skirt around the salt-flats, and arrive at the boat that had been made ready for his escape. He heard the sound of the bugler coming to him from the fort, and saw them forming into ranks, and heard the thump of their boots on the ground as they came to attention for roll-call.

(The way is clear and you've got to get a move on.)

He leaned over with his thin body and moved stealthily, his hand stretched ahead over the ground, his eyes taking in everything. He lowered his body, hiding behind the single fig tree and stayed concealed with his terror in the grip of the sands and the scaly rocks.

He thought about his companions who had all fled. He wondered what had happened to them. From the pictures that followed one another in succession, cuttingly sharp, he had the fear that they had been mowed down by bullets or had been sucked into the salt-flats.

(The boat is the way of escape.)

He crawled along the sand. When he saw he was drawing near to the sea he felt happy at his good fortune. He was being driven by his active imagination, his fevered memories, and a sense of unease.

He went back to the memory of passing through the door of the ancient building in the city's ancient suburb, after leaving the suburban train and ascending the stairs in a dreamlike frenzy. Rapping at the door, it was opened to him to show the face of a young girl in jeans, a sparkle in her eyes and a welcoming smile on her lips.

"Hello."

"Hello."

"They're all here?"

"All of them."

They were gathered around a table in their usual attire, with their unruly hair, agitated facial muscles, and their dream of a justice soon to be achieved. They were infatuated to a degree that recognized no adversity; they believed, and they were standing in the large room of the distant house in the suburb listening to the wild wind that never ceased blowing from afar. Soon they were leaning over the table, checking out what they were about. Everything in those days was accomplished in fine fashion. The vision was clear and they were all dreaming of it.

"The dream! What do you have left of it?" He uttered these words as he crawled forward on his stomach, with numbers of sand grouse scattering in alarm, circling around and flapping their wings aimlessly, their leader confused and agitated.

"Where are they now?" he asked himself.

The ground in front of him looked particularly harsh and uninviting. The silence had thickened within calling distance. The wind too had become silent, as had the soldiers' laughter.

An autumn evening, the boat on the water, and his dream, with which he would cross over the place of death to that other place where everything was not lost.

The fort looked even more featureless. He saw it as a sketch in an old book. He had drawn too close to the boat, more than

221

was safe. He would try to find his fortune elsewhere, but they were there, concealed inside the boat, patient and wholly silent.

When he saw them he stood up motionless. He did not attempt to flee, felt no fear. He did not know why it was that at this instant he remembered the girl who had opened the door of the house in the distant suburb and heard her voice coming from bottomless distances—"Hello, they're all here."

He regarded the soldiers as they fired in a single volley.

He fell to the ground.

The sky had become more overcast, its fiery sun concentrated into a single radiation of light. It began gradually to be quenched, slowly before his eyes, while he was conscious of the retreat of his soul from his body. As he lay there he would have liked to weep, but he was watching the waves being pulled back from the shore and moving away. Voices began to reach him from far off, from the lines of obscure books, the commingling of times, the loss of dreams as they strove to emerge from a memory that was dying. As he tried to cling to the last flicker of light, he saw the boat on the water being drawn away by the waves. On board was the smiling girl who had been standing at the door of the house in the suburbs.

Presence of the Absent Man

Alia Mamdouh

A nd another day . . .

    (This evening will have a different taste.)

    Since early morning the woman had been constantly walking about, on the move. She washed the passageway leading to the small garden in which were rows of sparse bushes, short, flaccid and drooping. She removed the cat from its shelter and took hold of one of the kittens. It tried to get away from her. It squatted on the ground, then gently let go its claws.

"Meiow . . . Meiow."

After she had cleaned the dirt from inside the small wooden shelter, she took hold of the mother cat and began talking to it. The cat's face bore that look that would turn to invective if the woman increased the amount of tenderness she was showing.

"Puss . . . Puss."

The woman is afflicted by a strange feeling of numbness. She fingers her wrinkled face and unties from her head the blue headscarf patterned with white and red circles. She takes it in her hand and folds it lengthways, then begins swinging it to right and left, playing with the kittens, while the mother cat looks on warily. The headscarf shakes between the woman's fingers, sometimes becoming the object of a tug-of-war in the teeth of one or other cat.

(Ah, I want to have someone to confide in.)

She leaves the door of the shelter open, and her face becomes grave with a certain sense of frustration and the dialogues she opens up with herself and for which she vainly waits for answers.

From morning she has been setting aside some of the furniture. This couch had not brought much luck: her husband had sat down on it and died. And this chair: whenever she sits on it, her thoughts become disrupted and she cannot say what she wants to say to those around her, a problem she does not know how to solve. What furniture, then, is left?

All she possesses are three bamboo chairs, a long sofa with rickety back legs, and another small one (which, however, is like a cavern in that whenever anyone sits in it they go off into a semi-trance). There is also an old carpet that covers quite a bit of the house, and curtains the color of dust that are in fact clean. Drawing back the curtains, she opens the large window that looks onto the garden. The cat is licking its kittens piled up on top of her like the gum that piles up over the fissures in a tree.

This evening she will be conversing with a real voice, and she trembles with delight. She leaves the window, enters her room, and extracts from a large, carefully wrapped bundle some white towels, a wooden comb with broad teeth, and a large cube-shaped cake of soap redolent with the scent of chicory. She looks at herself in the mirror: A woman in her forties, tall and with a dark complexion, sturdily built, her black hair slightly coarse, her muscles strong, giving the impression of severity, her eyes black and sharp, bespeaking a certain wildness. Carrying all her things, she puts them down on a small chair with short legs outside the bathroom door.

(Oh, if only I had some girl, I'd call her to gather up all these things for me, and I'd leave her standing outside until I came out of the bathroom.)

She quickly takes off her clothes. Despite herself, and with an unhurried movement, she looks with distaste at all the parts of her body. The bathroom was the sole place where she would gasp and cry out, not troubling to hide her embarrassment at seeing herself. Nor would she shrink from admitting that she had begun to age.

She opens the tap and hot tongues descend. The steam from the hot water dazes her and she begins first of all to scrub her face.

On her wedding night she had scrubbed her face so hard with some sort of stone that she had made it bleed. They told her it would fill the vessels of her face with pure, healthy blood. They also told her that a red face would be a green light for the man to satisfy all her desires. But while her face had continued to be radiant, luck had held aloof.

She scrubs her back with a piece of wood in the shape of a hand, moaning and laughing. She will remain a respectable woman, for no one expects her to be otherwise.

It was on her last visit to the big market: every Thursday the big market rises up in her head like the Prophet's Midnight Journey, and the new things she imagines she will be wearing cling to her mind, and the unknown man who will while away her time from home to market in the expectancy of something, and all the possibilities she used to see as impossible she would imagine as happening with every visit to the big market.

It was there that she saw her. A star in her haughtiness, obscenely and insolently beautiful. Her *abaya* gave out a revealing light, through which she quivered like someone who has lost her way. She was gazing in all directions; then, at last, her eyes came to rest on hers. When, suddenly, she bumped into her, the *abaya* fell down from a head that trembled with shyness and a face that veered between recalcitrance and chastity. "I didn't mean to embarrass you."

The other woman did not reply. She remained silent, innocent, alarmed about something that was going to occur. Leaning forward, she became, amid that throng of people, a ball being hurled about by buyers and sellers. And when the other opened her arms and quickly clasped her, fearful she would fall, the two of them looked at each other. The two pairs of eyes were pierced by the light from a match that had just been struck, and the two bodies released a blaze of high tension, while between their fingers crept cold, damp sweat.

"Every Thursday I come here—and you?"

The other woman did not reply.

"I've not seen you before. Are you from here?"

Like a sting, gripped by what was around her, the other woman answers, "I'm on a visit."

"Anyone with you?"

"My husband and the children are waiting for me at the entrance to the market."

How was it that she had not seen this face before, this reticent, alert, suspicious face, a face made for passion? When she proceeded to free herself from her, she clung to her, saying—the words all mixed up with the voices of vendors, the screaming of children, the clamor of women doing their shopping, and the mewing of cats standing far off waiting for somewhere to take shelter—"Every Thursday I come here."

And her voice was lost amid the din of passers-by.

But the other woman takes herself off like hallowed sin, and all these scenes evaporate and she is moving about alone, with despair gathering inside her head like a hemorrhage.

Her eyes are half-closed, and the soap flows over her pores, the bubbles losing themselves on the naked brown flesh. She stretches out her legs, the brown froth bespattered on her knees.

(First of all I'll look into her eyes, and then I'll get to know her. I want to be sure she's in front of me, for the time between looking at someone and getting to know them is a new departure.)

She wants to begin from her toes. She will tickle them first, so as to see her smile. Maybe she will cry out with joy: joy is like death, and for her nothing but death remains.

She leans against the bathroom wall and sings an old folk song. She places her dirty clothes in an ancient washbowl, scouring them with her hand while continuing to sing.

And she will seat her in front of her and at first will look into her eyes and will not wait for any sign of the screen being raised. Like her, she will be on her own.

She will bring the food for the cat and its kittens so that their mewing will not disturb them, and she will put all the clocks out of action and will sit waiting for her like a child waiting for its New Year present.

She squeezes out her clothes.

(First of all I'll squeeze her knees, because the only time I saw her knees they looked like two solitary fruits on a lofty tree.)

She leans against the wall for a while.

She will not put on the strong light, so she will not be suddenly startled.

She stands upright in the middle of the bathroom and her shadow looks solid and solitary.

The breasts are heavy, the shoulders broad, the hips full, the thighs taut. The hair falls sedately down to the neck; the neck

227

itself is smooth, the face giving itself up completely to becoming, after a while, the half-circle that will become complete with the semicircle that will shortly be coming.

On the second Thursday she did not come, neither on the third, the fourth, the fifth, or the sixth. She would hurry to the market, with the noon heat approaching fifty degrees. Her eyes would be bloodshot, her stomach saturated with the smell of sweat and that physical desire she did not want to be dispersed after having come so close to it.

She would hurl herself at the vendors, shouting unreasonably about the rise in prices, then buying unnecessary things. A cat crouched against the wall, its tongue dry, its body ablaze with the heat. At home the cat stays for days without food: in retribution for all these times of dejection, she deprives the cat and its kittens of food. She looks at herself in the mirror.

(I've aged six weeks all at once.)

She had not got to know her name, and all names were jostling in her head in a nightmare. She did not know her address and all addresses took turns in destroying her because of her separation from her.

They had come to know one another in a feverish manner. Every morning she would pile up the sheets on the floor, throw the pillows against the wall, strike her head with a fierce blow of her fist, and tell herself that she was emotionally bankrupt.

After the first meeting she stayed a week without washing, lest the other woman's signature be erased from her body, and every Thursday would bring her defeat and the ordeal of futile hopes.

When, once again, she seats herself on the wooden sofa, she curls her legs into a triangle, lets down her hair, and begins combing it. The smell of henna and infused chicory, the steam from the hot water, the female presence, all impose themselves strongly on her: she wants to remain alive, youthful, desirable.

(We shall be alone and no one will have any suspicions about us. The neighbors will say she's my woman friend, and the vendors at the souk will catch their breath when she arrives there.)

Anyone hearing her humming to herself would think that Paradise was being taken by storm, and anyone seeing her coming out of the bathroom daubed with silky perfume would know that she will shortly be betrothed: a woman concealed behind a black childhood, a naive adolescence, and an uncourageous youth.

She is a woman who has wallowed in grief and become liable to collapse but who had not wanted to mutilate her life, had wanted neither to disappear like so much vapor nor to shine like some star; she is beginning to become capable of achieving continuity with some creature, be it a cat, a spider, a woman, even a jungle animal or a snake.

And this place of banishment, what magically gaudy toys it has, and what despair to make captive the heart and body, and what a way by which to attain tranquillity.

On the seventh Thursday she quivered like the short-branched pomegranate tree as she looked into the face of the other woman, a face that was wax-white.

"Do you want to go to the back street?"

They walked together, two specters that had grown weary through remembering and love-sickness, two visible, waking beings dazzled by the infernal fire that they would shortly be entering. They came to a stop and the passers-by around them were like the vibrations of a radio tuner that is caught between two stations.

"The very evening I left you my husband left me."

This penetrating blackness was slowly flowing out of the night, and objects ceased to come between them; fear, this taboo that was spread between them, did not touch them. They were two beings without equal.

"And the children?"

"I left them at my mother's."

"And you?"

"I want you."

She took her hand. When they were apart she used to say to herself: So everything's been revealed, but now everything's begun.

On the seventh Thursday hands will touch with greater sweetness. She took her by the hand and they walked in the back street and boarded the large bus and sat together.

"I want to touch you now."

"No, not now."

She pointed to her house and got off. The total moment will come, and she will recollect with what bashfulness people had previously encircled her. For several years she had been pierced through with trembling, and she had chased it away as white corpuscles chase away germs. The blood, though, had not been poisoned and would, once again, gush forth, carrying with it all these accumulations of emotions. All this life that has passed is a falsehood, all that aged history a falsehood, and absurd those small alliances that begin in one place and end in another.

Slowly she turns her head in the room and sits drying her body. An unspoken question seizes hold of her. What if she refuses, what if she bids her farewell by withdrawing into herself?

What a stratagem it is that comes about from a clash of fires! Hurriedly she rises and puts on a long red woolen nightdress. After squeezing her hair dry, she allows it to fall down to her shoulders. She sinks onto the couch. The smell of the bath, filled with soap, henna, and chicory, permeates the room like a sort of incense.

The gown is easy to pull off, the nightdress long, with buttons at the breast and nothing more.

Suddenly she hears the door open and then close quietly without banging. "Who is it?"

The other woman peers around the doorway.

"You?"

"Me."

Her face is grief-stricken, defeated, as though she has emerged from a snare. She remains standing. She takes in all the objects with an all-embracing glance. She throws her *abaya* to the ground and seats herself on it. She leans against the wall and takes a deep breath: it seems to her that the room has become so restricted it is turning into a tomb, while the woman is still on the sofa, as silent as an angel in panic.

Thus they remain, speechless for more than several minutes, their breathing constricted, not knowing where things will start or how the evening will turn out. Both of them are frightened, as the woman sits on the floor, her knees cracking, her face paralyzed by fever, and she herself turns her head slowly and casts apprehensive yet conclusive glances at the earthly creature sitting close by her.

The anticipation of this moment is the contract binding this sublime partnership. Is not everything in the end mere desires, with which we adorn these unions that we can put into effect only in dreams?

The mewing of the cat increases the nervousness of the two women.

"What a noise—it's hungry."

How can they say that the body gets pensioned off? This mucus locked within the gullet and the veins, from where does it come? And the cat's saliva, does it not have a sanguine nerve? What incompatibility is there between the prick of a pin and the whiplashes of thoughts? What is the significance of a great victory over a small force? She believes that the discovery of magic is more powerful than magic itself, and all of a sudden she rises to her feet and at that moment it seems to her that embarking upon magic is the bringing together of the small particles that are entangled inside her. She seats herself on the floor close to the other woman, and the mewing outside begins to break up this small pleasure. What honor is this that she herself will know of and what hellish temptation leads the two of them to revolt?— and the cat, with its proficiency at continuing to diminish the elation, is peering through the window with hurt eyes and a madly brandishing tail.

Thirst and the quenching of it, hunger and satiety, night and morning, birth and death, flight and presence. What a dark coming together despite the harmony of it!

"Did you pass by the children?"

"I visited them before coming here."

"And him?"

"The So-and-so got himself married right away."

"He didn't tell you why?"

"Yes—don't you see what I look like now? He dislikes pregnant women."

"And are you miserable?"

"Very."

"But why? Did you love him all that much?"

She grew pale. Love stays only for a little while, and banal endings become frozen, as do the big disappointments; and so that people may come to know one another without any law, everything is expressed through pallor.

The woman continues what she had to say. "But I . . ."

Her pulse beats harder, the cat's mewing rains down, and this continuous pricking has afflicted the three faces: two women whose bodies reveal a certain plumpness and a cat that invents kinds of clamor designed to bring it security.

"I still think of him. You don't know how he used to watch me when I was among people, and when we were on our own, and how he used to rule over me, and how he would control me. O sister mine—man is a beautiful curse that we cannot pretend to do without. Look at this dress, he bought it for me before the break-up and said to me jokingly, 'Make it so that it can be taken off quickly'—and so many other things."

"That's enough, enough, enough."

The maddening mewing, the throbbing heartbeats, the sudden irritation, the memories that have followed without interruption for the last hour, the long moments of frustration, the cat's thirst, the woman's pain, and the force of this aggression among the three of them.

She turns toward the window, looks at the cat triumphantly. The cat is scrutinizing the two of them. The other woman takes hold of her *abaya*, drawing it out from under her, and sits comfortably. The rustling of her dress sighs with this naked joy. She radiates beams of light.

She murmurs between her teeth, "How close you are to me: your arm is like his, your muscles strong like his, your glances overflowing with this frenzied inferno." Shifting backward, she raises her head to the light. The cat renews its mewings. A white line gleams between mouth and mouth, and the lips mumble words. The cat bursts through the glass of the window and enters, covered in blood and bringing with it cravings of hunger and thirst.

About the Authors

YUSUF ABU RAYYA was born in the town of Hihya in the Nile Delta and studied journalism at Cairo University. For some years he worked on various newspapers and magazines. He was then awarded a period of three years to concentrate on his writing. Since then he has produced two novels and a volume of short stories, as well as a novel for children. Some of his stories have appeared in German translation.

IBRAHIM ASLAN, born in the Nile Delta in 1939, failed to complete his secondary education and is largely self-taught. At present he is the Cairo correspondent for the prestigious Lebanese daily paper *al-Hayat* and is also responsible for a series of government paperback reprints of writing from all over the Arab world. Though he has published only three volumes of short stories and two novels, he is regarded as one of Egypt's most talented writers. His novel *The Heron* was made into one of the most successful Arabic films. His recently published novel *Nile Sparrows* was critically acclaimed.

HANA ATIA, born in Cairo, took a degree at the Pyramids Academy of Arts in cinema techniques and has written several screenplays. She has made a name for herself as a writer of short stories, of which she has published three volumes. She has also written a novel which is about to be published. Several of her stories have been published in French and Norwegian translations.

ABDULLAH BAKHSHAWEEN was born in al-Ta'if in western Saudi Arabia in 1953. His family was poor, so he was unable to continue his formal education beyond primary level, and began working at the age of thirteen in a variety of menial jobs. In 1970 he began his writing career as a journalist on local papers, then spent six years in Iraq working for a magazine. His first collection of short stories was published in 1986, his second in 1998. He has also written two novels.

SALWA BAKR, born in Cairo, made her name with her first book of short stories, which she published at her own expense. Since then a selection of her stories translated into English by Denys Johnson-Davies has been published under the title *The Wiles of Men*, and she has written several novels, including *The Golden Chariot*, which is also available in English translation. Her work has been translated into several other languages and is particularly popular with German readers. Her most recent work is a two-volume historical novel about the uprising of Coptic Egypt against Islamic rule in the ninth century.

MOHAMED EL-BISATIE was born in 1938 in a Nile Delta village overlooking Lake Manzala. Having left there to go to university in Cairo, he has never felt the desire to return, though most of his writings are about the area of his childhood. Since 1968 he has published seven volumes of short stories and eight novels.

A representative volume of his short stories, translated by the Denys Johnson-Davies, was published in Cairo and America under the title *The Last Glass of Tea*. His novel *Houses Behind the Trees*, recently made into a film in Egypt, was also published in an English translation by the same translator. Retired from government service, he is now chief editor of a series of paper-backs issued under the title *Literary Voices*.

BRAHIM DARGOUTHI was born in southern Tunisia in 1955 and graduated from the Teachers' College in Tunis. He has worked as a teacher and is now a headmaster. He has published four nov-els and four collections of short stories. Three of his novels have been translated into French and one into German. He has been awarded several literary prizes.

GAMAL AL-GHITANI was born in 1945 in a village in Upper Egypt and grew up in the Gamaliya district of old Cairo. He first studied oriental carpet design. Like many Egyptian intellectuals he spent time in detention for political activity. He worked as a war corre-spondent, and since 1985 has been employed as a literary journal-ist and is presently editor of the influential weekly *Akhbar al-adab*. His short stories have been widely published in Arab and Egyptian periodicals. His work has been published in ten languages; in English he is best known for his novel *Zayni Barakat*. He has received various prizes including the State Prize for the Novel.

ABDOU GUBEIR was born in 1950 in a small town on the banks of the Nile in Upper Egypt. Coming from a religious family, he was destined for a career as a muezzin or a preacher in a mosque. At the age of fourteen, however, he decided he wanted to be a writer and escaped to Cairo where he worked at a variety of jobs. This period of his life provided material for his most recent novel,

Radwan's Vacation. He works on a daily newspaper in Kuwait and plans to return to Egypt shortly in order to devote himself to creative writing. He has published two volumes of short stories and three novels; he is now at work on a novel about Egyptians who go to the Gulf states in search of work.

GHALIB HALASA was born in Jordan in 1932 and died in 1989 in Syria. His active pro-Palestinian politics caused him to lead an interrupted life in many Arab capitals, including Beirut, Damascus, and Baghdad. He also spent many years in Cairo, from which he was expelled in 1976. His writings were highly regarded and include seven novels and two volumes of short stories. He translated several books from English and published a number of critical studies.

YUSUF IDRIS was born in 1927 and died in London in 1991. He published his first collection of short stories in 1954, with an introduction by the eminent man of letters Taha Hussein. This established him as a writer with unique talents and as the undisputed master of the short story in Arabic. Having qualified as a doctor, his experiences as a private practitioner and a government health inspector provided him with the material for many of his most famous stories. A concern for the underprivileged and a political consciousness underlies most of his writing, whether it be short stories or plays, a genre in which he also excelled. Two volumes of his short stories have been published in English translation, as well as his novel *City of Love and Ashes*.

INAAM KACHACHI, born in Baghdad, has lived in Paris since 1979 where she works as a journalist. She has published several short stories, and a book about Lorna Hales, the British artist who was married to Iraq's leading sculptor Jawad Selim.

SAID AL-KAFRAWI was born in the Delta of Egypt, and most of his stories are devoted to village life. In his writing he has confined himself to the short story, of which he has published seven volumes. A representative collection of his stories in English, translated by Denys Johnson-Davies, appeared in 1998 under the title *The Hill of Gypsies*. Individual stories have been translated into several European languages. At present he works in the Cairo office of the Kuwaiti magazine *al-Arabi*.

EDWAR AL-KHARRAT was born in 1926 in Alexandria and studied law at Alexandria University. For some years he worked as the deputy secretary-general of the Afro-Asian Writers' Association. His first book, a volume of short stories, was published at his own expense in 1959. Since then he has written prolifically and has produced a large number of volumes of short stories and novels. He has also been an active translator from English and French. Two of his recent novels, *The City of Saffron* and *Girls of Alexandria*, are available in English translation. He has been awarded the prestigious Owais Prize for his contribition to Arabic literature and more recently the 1999 Naguib Mahfouz Medal for Literature for his novel *Rama and the Dragon*, which is currently being translated into English. An autobiographical book won the Mémoires de la Mediterranée Prize and will appear translated into six European languages.

MOHAMED KHUDAYIR was born near Basra in southern Iraq, where he works as a schoolmaster. He has published three volumes of short stories, and a work entitled *Basriyata* about the town in which he lives. Despite his small output he is regarded as one of the outstanding talents practicing the short story. Another of his stories appears in the collection *Arabic Short Stories*, translated by Denys Johnson-Davies.

IBRAHIM AL-KONI was born in 1948 in Ghadames, Libya, to Touareg parents. He graduated from the Gorki Institute in Moscow and has held several senior governmental positions both in Libya and in Warsaw and Moscow. He presently lives in the Swiss Alps and devotes himself wholly to writing. He has published more than thirty books, including volumes of short stories, novels, and collections of essays and criticism. His work has been widely published in translation and he has been awarded various literary prizes.

NAGUIB MAHFOUZ was born in the district of Gamaliya in Cairo, an area in which much of his writing, including his famous *Trilogy*, is set. He worked in various government posts until his retirement in 1972. He began his writing career early, with his first novel published in 1939. Since then he has written over thirty novels and more than a hundred short stories. Many of his novels have been made into successful films. In 1988 his career was crowned with the award of the Nobel Prize for Literature. Much of his writing is available today in English translation. Denys Johnson-Davies has translated several books by Mahfouz, including a selection of his short stories under the title *The Time and the Place*.

MOHAMED MAKHZANGI was born in 1950 in the town of Mansoura in the Delta of Egypt. He studied to become a doctor and later specialised in psychology and alternative medicine in the Ukrainian capital Kiev. Having worked for some time as a doctor, he turned to writing and journalism, and worked in Kuwait on the magazine *al-Arabi,*. Besides five volumes of short stories, he has published a literary examination of the Chernobyl atomic disaster, which he himself lived through. Translations of his stories have also appeared in French, German, Russian, and Chinese. Having left Kuwait, he now lives between Egypt and Syria.

ALIA MAMDOUH was born in Baghdad. After taking a degree in psychology, she became the editor of an Iraqi independent weekly, until she left Baghdad in 1982. She moved to Beirut, thence to Tunis, and so to Morocco, where she lived from 1983 to 1990, working on the editorial staff of various newspapers and magazines. Her novel *Mothballs* has appeared in translations in English, French, Italian, German, Spanish, Dutch, and Catalan. She now lives in Paris.

ABD AL-AZIZ MISHRI was born in 1955 in al-Baha province, Saudi Arabia. With only a preparatory school certificate, he went on to work on a local newspaper before devoting himself full-time to his writing career. During a short life beset by illness, he published five collections of short stories and three novels. He was also known as a painter and illustrator. He died in early 2000.

BUTHAYNA AL-NASIRI was born in Baghdad and took a degree in English literature from Baghdad University. Her first volume of short stories was published in 1974, and four more volumes have appeared since then. Her stories have been translated into English, German, French, Spanish, and Danish. She currently lives in Cairo.

IBRAHIM SAMOUIEL was born in Damascus in 1951. Since earning a degree in philosophy and psychology, he has been employed as a social worker with disabled persons and young delinquents. He has specialised in the short story, of which he has published four volumes. One of his volumes has appeared in Italian, while individual stories have been translated into English, French, and Chinese.

SALMA MATAR SEIF is the nom de plume of a writer of short stories from Ajman, one of the smaller states of the United Arab Emirates. She works as a government employee in the sphere of education and is studying for her MA from an Egyptian university. She has published three volumes of short stories and is at present working on a novel.

KHAIRY SHALABY is one of Egypt's best known and most prolific writers, having published a half dozen volumes of short stories and more than ten novels, as well as travel books and volumes of criticism. Among his best known works is his long novel *Wikalat Atiya*, which was voted the best novel of 1993 and is at present being translated into French. Two of his novels have been translated into English and individual stories have appeared in Russian and Chinese. Several of his works have been adapted for television and the screen.

HANAN AL-SHAYKH was born in southern Lebanon but lived most of her early life in Beirut. She attended the American College for Girls in Cairo, where, at the age of twenty-one, she wrote her first novel. Returning to Beirut, she worked on a women's magazine and for the literary supplement of the leading daily paper *al-Nahar*. With marriage, she moved with her husband to Saudi Arabia, where she lived for several years and wrote her second novel. Her third book, *The Story of Zahra*, was translated into English and established her as one of the few Arab novelists with a worldwide reputation. Her other novels include *Women of Sand and Myrrh* and *Beirut Blues*. She has also published volumes of short stories. She presently lives in London.

FUAD AL-TAKARLI, was born in Baghdad in 1927. He graduated from Law College and was appointed a judge in 1956, continuing in that post until 1983. He published his first collection of short stories in 1960. His first novel, *The Long Way Back*, was published in Beirut in 1980 and has been translated into French; an English translation is currently in preparation. In 1995 he published another novel and in 1999 he was awarded the prestigious Owais Prize. Having lived in Paris for several years, he has now settled in Tunis.

ZAKARIA TAMER was born in Damascus in 1929 and received little formal education. He immediately established himself as a new voice in the field of the short story with the publication in the 1960s of his first volume, *The Neighing of the White Steed.* His writings for children also enjoy success. In Damascus he held various government posts before going abroad to work on an Arabic newspaper published in London. A selection of his stories in English translation by Denys Johnson-Davies appeared in 1985 under the title *Tigers on the Tenth Day.* He currently lives in Oxford, England.

MAHMOUD AL-WARDANI was born in Cairo in 1950. He began writing shortly after leaving university and has published three volumes of short stories and four novels. His stories have appeared in English and German translations. He spent periods in prison for political reasons, but has also represented Egypt at literary conventions in the Arab world and Europe. He currently works as a senior editor on Cairo's weekly literary magazine *Akhbar al-Adab.*

AMINA ZAYDAN was born in Suez. She took a degree in commerce and works locally in the Ministry of Finance. She has published two volumes of short stories and a novel. Her first book, the title story of which is included in the present volume, won first prize in a competition held by the literary magazine *Akhbar al-Adab*. She is at present engaged on her second novel which deals with those people in the Suez area who were forced to vacate their homes during the tripartite attack on Egypt in 1956.

MOHAMED ZEFZAF is one of Morocco's leading writers and lives in Casablanca, where he has worked as a schoolteacher. He has published nine collections of short stories and nine novels. His short stories have been widely translated and several of his novels have appeared in Spanish, French, and Russian translations.

DENYS JOHNSON-DAVIES was born in Vancouver and spent his youth in Sudan and East Africa. Having studied Arabic at Cambridge and London Universities, he worked variously with the BBC Arabic section, as a lecturer at Cairo University, as director of an Arabic broadcasting station in the Gulf, and as a barrister in London. He is regarded as the pioneer translator of modern Arabic literature, but he is also interested in Islamic studies and is cotranslator of three volumes of Prophetic Hadith. His adaptation of a fourteenth-century fable by the Brethren of Purity, under the title *The Island of Animals* and with an introduction about Islam's attitude toward the treatment of animals, revealed his interest in the subject of man's responsibility toward his fellow creatures. His most recent translation, from al-Ghazali's *Ihya 'ulum al-Din*, about manners relating to eating, was published in 2000 by the Islamic Texts Society. Other publications include some fifteen books for children adapted from Arabic sources. A volume of his own short stories, *Fate of a Prisoner*, was published in 1999 and has appeared in an Arabic translation.

Modern Arabic Literature
from the American University in Cairo Press

Ibrahim Abdel Meguid *Birds of Amber*
No One Sleeps in Alexandria • The Other Place
Yahya Taher Abdullah *The Mountain of Green Tea*
Leila Abouzeid *The Last Chapter*
Hamdi Abu Golayyel *Thieves in Retirement*
Yusuf Abu Rayya *Wedding Night*
Ahmed Alaidy *Being Abbas el Abd*
Idris Ali *Dongola: A Novel of Nubia • Poor*
Ibrahim Aslan *The Heron • Nile Sparrows*
Alaa Al Aswany *The Yacoubian Building*
Fadhil al-Azzawi *The Last of the Angels*
Hala El Badry *A Certain Woman • Muntaha*
Salwa Bakr *The Man from Bashmour • The Wiles of Men*
Hoda Barakat *Disciples of Passion • The Tiller of Waters*
Mourid Barghouti *I Saw Ramallah*
Mohamed El-Bisatie *Clamor of the Lake • Houses Behind the Trees*
A Last Glass of Tea • Over the Bridge
Mansoura Ez Eldin *Maryam's Maze*
Ibrahim Farghali *The Smiles of the Saints*
Hamdy el-Gazzar *Black Magic*
Fathy Ghanem *The Man Who Lost His Shadow*
Randa Ghazy *Dreaming of Palestine*
Gamal al-Ghitani *Pyramid Texts • Zayni Barakat*
Yahya Hakki *The Lamp of Umm Hashim*
Bensalem Himmich *The Polymath • The Theocrat*
Taha Hussein *The Days • A Man of Letters • The Sufferers*
Sonallah Ibrahim *Cairo: From Edge to Edge • The Committee • Zaat*
Yusuf Idris *City of Love and Ashes*
Denys Johnson-Davies *The AUC Press Book of Modern Arabic Literature*
Under the Naked Sky: Short Stories from the Arab World
Said al-Kafrawi *The Hill of Gypsies*
Sahar Khalifeh *The End of Spring • The Image, the Icon, and the Covenant*
The Inheritance